Racing Fear

Racing Fear

Jacqueline Guest

James Lorimer & Company Ltd., Publishers
Toronto

FIC
GUE

First publication in the United States, 2004

James Lorimer & Company Ltd. acknowledges the support of
the Ontario Arts Council. We acknowledge the support of the
Government of Canada through the Book Publishing Industry
Development Program (BPIDP) for our publishing activities.
We acknowledge the support of the Canada Council for the
Arts for our publishing program. We acknowledge the sup-
port of the Government of Ontario through the Ontario Media
Development Corporation's Ontario Book Initiative.

The Canada Council | Le Conseil des Arts
for the Arts | du Canada

ONTARIO ARTS COUNCIL
CONSEIL DES ARTS DE L'ONTARIO

Cover design: Clarke MacDonald

National Library of Canada Cataloguing in Publication

Guest, Jacqueline
    Racing fear / written by Jacqueline Guest.

(SideStreets)
ISBN 1-55028-839-3 (bound)   ISBN 1-55028-838-5 (pbk.)

    I. Title. II. Series.

PS8563.U365R32 2004   jC813'.54   C2004-900480-8

James Lorimer
& Company Ltd.,
Publishers
35 Britain Street
Toronto, Ontario
M5A 1R7
www.lorimer.ca

Distributed in the United States by:
Orca Book Publishers,
P.O. Box 468
Custer, WA USA
98240-0468

Printed and bound in Canada

Acknowledgements:

I'd like to thank the following people for their invaluable help:

Dr. C.L. LeBlanc, Shawn Bishop and the Calgary Sports Car Club, and especially Jorge Dascollas for explaining how rally drivers make the magic happen.

—Jacqueline Guest
www.jacquelineguest.com

Prologue

The steering wheel shudders violently under Adam's hands. Salty sweat burns his eyes. He came into the corner way too hot.

His eyes dart to his passenger. He wishes again that he made Trent fasten his seat belt.

He knows the car is understeering, sliding dangerously close to the edge of the embankment. Adam lifts his foot off the accelerator, allowing the car to tuck in and make the corner.

His knuckles whiten. The car isn't responding. It's still heading straight for the cliff and he can't stop it!

Adam's heart pounds in his chest as the front wheels reach the edge. The car seems to hang in space for an instant, then loses the fight and gives itself over to the darkness.

Terror squeezes the air out of Adam's lungs as the car flies like a blind bird into the empty expanse. He braces himself for the impact.

With a bone-rending screech of twisting metal, the car slams into the rocks below and begins tearing itself apart.

Blackness drags Adam down until the searing pain is released and he feels nothing.

The last sounds he hears are Trent's terrible screams.

Chapter 1

Gasping for air, Adam sat bolt upright. Faint grey streaks tinged the edge of the early morning clouds. He wiped the sweat off his forehead.

Climbing out of bed, Adam moved silently down the hallway to the bathroom and splashed cold water on his face. He looked in the mirror, hardly recognizing the gaunt reflection that stared back at him. His sunken eyes were shadowed and felt like they'd been ground into gravel. His cropped brown hair was damp as though he had a fever, and his lean body felt stiff from muscles that had been tensed all night.

He'd been having the same gut-wrenching nightmare for months and it was killing him.

He dressed and went downstairs to make something to eat; going back to bed was out of the question. He was listlessly smearing blueberry cream cheese on his toasted bagel when his parents walked into the kitchen.

"Good morning, sweetheart." His mother kissed the top of his head as she greeted him.

"Coffee smells great." Pouring himself a steaming cup, his dad topped up Adam's mug, then glanced at his son. "Still having trouble sleeping?"

Adam knew his appearance was a dead giveaway to his dad. They'd talked about Adam's dreams before. "A little," he admitted, the memories flooding back.

It had all started nine months ago here in Calgary. Adam and his best friend, Trent Kendall, had been joy riding in a rally car borrowed without permission from Trent's dad. Both of them were heavily into road rallying and were always competing against each other, forever trying to clip the apex on a corner a little more precisely or shave one extra second off a special stage.

When Trent had bet Adam couldn't drive the opening section of the most recent Kananaskis Rally, Adam had laughed and taken the bet. They'd headed into Alberta's Rocky Mountains and the huge track of land that was the Kananaskis Forest Reserve. Neither of them suspected what was waiting in the darkness.

"Adam, you have to ease up on yourself." His father's voice startled him, interrupting his thoughts. "You were only sixteen. Lots of new drivers underestimate the power of their cars and don't react properly when they get into trouble. I'm sure it was the old story of too much ego and too little experience."

Adam sipped his coffee and tried once more to explain to his father and to himself why he deserved to be tortured every night with the spectre of the deadly crash. "Dad, I can't *ease up*. Don't you see — the accident was my fault. I couldn't handle the car. I failed and Trent paid the price." He set his cup down a little too hard, spilling the coffee onto the tablecloth. "I walked away with hardly a scratch, while Trent nearly died!"

Adam remembered burning the blood-soaked clothes he'd worn that night, hoping to burn the terrible memory with them. Instead, it had seared the images into his brain, leaving their dark imprint to haunt his nightmares.

"Maybe you feel guilty because you never had a chance to say goodbye to Trent before we left," his mother interjected. "That wasn't your fault either, honey. If I remember correctly, you tried to see him but the hospital wouldn't let you."

Adam knew both his parents were trying to help. The timing of their move to Saudi Arabia couldn't have been worse. Adam knew that his parents had felt bad when, immediately after the accident, the oil company Adam's dad worked for transferred him.

Adam wasn't able to say goodbye to Trent, who was still in intensive care. He wouldn't have known what to say to his friend anyway.

Now his dad had received a promotion and, as suddenly as they had moved away, they were back in Calgary. That had been a week ago.

"Once you two start talking again, I'm sure it will help. You're going to see Trent today, right?" his mom asked.

"Yeah, Zoë called and said Trent heard I was back and wants to see me." It worried Adam that Trent's sister had been the one to call, not Trent himself. He took a deep breath, but his hands shook as he reached for his abandoned cup again.

His dad put a gentle hand on Adam's shoulder. "I'm sure Trent doesn't hold you responsible or he wouldn't be trying to get back together. Relax and stop borrowing trouble. Go see your old friend."

His father's reassuring touch eased the tightness in Adam's chest and he took another calming breath. "Sure, Dad. I'll let you two know how it goes."

He tried to sound like it was no big deal, but the truth was that even thinking about the accident made him break out in a cold sweat. He'd tried to get past it; in fact, riding in cars with anyone else didn't bother him. It was only when he remembered *that* night and *that* car and *all that blood*... The guilt at what he'd done to his best friend felt as crushing as the falling car.

Today, he would have to force himself to get past that guilt. Today, for the first time since the accident, he would face Trent Kendall.

* * *

14

"Well, hello, stranger!" Zoë Kendall's bright smile lit up her face as she opened the elaborately carved wooden door. She had grown considerably taller since Adam had seen her last. He was nearly six feet tall, and she had no trouble looking him squarely in the eye.

While both sets of parents had talked to settle the insurance details from the accident, Adam hadn't tried to contact the Kendalls at all and was now embarrassed for not calling. "Hi, Zoë. It's been a while. Hey, I'm sorry I never got in touch, but..." He ran his hand through his short hair as he searched for the right excuse. "Communications in Saudi are the pits. We were still going through the red tape involved in getting e-mail set up when we left, and I've been crazy busy since we got back..." He stopped, knowing his excuses sounded lame.

"Don't worry about apologizing to me, Adam Harlow!" she laughed. "It's big brother Trent you're going to have to grovel to." She led him to the solarium of the huge Kendall house.

As a criminal defence lawyer and a senior partner for a successful law firm, Trent's dad pulled down mega-bucks, but the Kendalls also came from "old money" and their family was very prominent in social circles. From the new Ferrari F50 sitting in the driveway, Adam decided Mr. Kendall knew exactly the right thing to do with that old money.

As they entered the sunny room, Trent was

standing with his back to them. He turned and Adam's stomach tightened. The long scar on his friend's face was a livid pink. It ran in a ragged line from Trent's jaw up to what was left of his right ear. His eyes were an odd washed-out green colour and now they appeared even paler next to the fiery scar.

"Hey, old buddy. Long time no see!" He started toward them, and Adam saw that Trent limped awkwardly on his left leg.

"Hi, Trent." Adam was going to spiel off his litany of excuses but, looking at his friend's torn face, he suddenly felt he couldn't. "I meant to call and we were trying to get e-mail over there, but the truth is, I suck and I'm sorry."

Trent frowned. "You're sorry because you've blown me off since the accident or you're sorry because you suck?" He laughed nervously and Adam realized that Trent was probably as freaked out about this meeting as he was.

"Both," Adam said sheepishly.

Trent moved a halting step closer. "It's okay. I'm the forgiving type. Besides, I've been kept pretty busy with the ladies. They love a man with a gory history. I'm like that Van Gogh guy who cut off his own ear." He tentatively touched his mangled ear as though he wasn't sure it belonged to him. "As for sucking, I can't do much for you on that score. Come to think of it, I doubt anyone could help you with that one, Harlow!" He motioned Adam to take a seat. "I'm really glad to see you. I couldn't believe it when Zoë said you'd called and were going to stop by."

Adam gave Zoë a questioning look. *She'd* been the one to call *him*, saying Trent had asked for this meeting.

Zoë grinned mischievously at him. "I'll get snacks while you two chat." She hurried out of the room before Adam could say anything.

"Come on, Adam, we've got some catching up to do." Trent flopped down onto a white wicker sofa as Adam moved to a big comfy-looking chair. "The old man said the cops figured totalling the car was an accident and there were no charges."

Adam leaned back. "Yeah, inexperience and poor road conditions added up to a no-fault crash. I was a pretty lucky guy."

At the word "lucky," Trent glanced over at Adam and raised his eyebrows. Adam felt his face redden.

Trent moved on. "After the accident, you escaped overseas before I had a chance to think straight. By the time I was out of the hospital, the old man saw to it I was kept way busy catching up with my schoolwork. He even hired a tutor so I wouldn't flunk out and embarrass him." Trent lifted his damaged leg onto a stool. "Like, as if I needed a tutor! That's just like my old man. His motto is 'if Trent has a problem, the best way to make it go away is to throw money at it.'"

Adam knew his friend was exceptionally smart, especially in chemistry, but didn't do well in school. Trent always said he hated the way his teachers taught, and thought he was smarter than a lot of them. Sometimes Trent's temper got in the way of his I.Q.

Adam suspected Mr. Kendall had simply hired the tutor to help his son catch up after he'd missed so much class time. But when it came to his dad's motives, Trent always thought the worst first.

Zoë returned with a big bowl of potato chips and soft drinks. She handed a can of pop to Adam. "Did I miss anything?"

"Trent was telling me about school." Relaxing a little, he cracked open the can.

"Let's say I haven't had much time to play." Trent took a long pull on his pop.

"Speaking of schools, I start at Springbank High on Monday. I don't think school in Saudi was up to the same level as here, which bites because I may have fallen seriously behind in a couple of subjects. If I can get back up to speed, I'll be finishing my grade twelve with the rest of you." Adam scrutinized the label on his pop can. "Looks like we'll be classmates again." Adam worried that, because of the accident, Trent wouldn't want to be around him, and going to the same school would make avoiding each other impossible.

"Hey, that's great! It will be like old times." Trent grabbed a handful of chips.

Yeah, right, Adam thought. How could anything be like old times ever again? The whole world had changed.

"How are your parents, Adam?" Zoë asked brightly.

"The same. We're back because dad got a promotion. He's been figuring out his new position while my mom decides what she wants to do. Everything happened so quickly, none of us is really over the jet lag yet. That's the reason I haven't called." He couldn't very well spill his guts and tell the truth, that Trent's mangled face was his fault.

"I know the real reason, Adam." Trent watched him intently. "It's because…"

Adam stopped, wondering if Trent had somehow guessed his secret. The can trembled in his hand.

"*You suck!*" Trent finished with a snort. "But I'm still glad you came over."

Adam laughed uneasily and took a noisy swallow of his pop.

"Did you tell Adam the big news?" Zoë asked as she reached for the chips.

"What big news?" Adam was grateful for the subject change. He tried not to stare at Trent's scar, but his gaze seemed to be drawn to the jagged gash like steel to a magnet.

Trent smiled at his sister. "I was getting to that, Zoë." His face became serious as he turned to his friend. "Adam, that lousy stint in the hospital had a silver lining. While I was there, the docs thought I was acting strange and decided to run some tests on me, then they asked my parents and teachers tons of questions. The tests came back with freakin' wild results." He began picking at the hem on the cushion.

Adam looked from Trent to Zoë, then back to Trent. "What results?"

Trent took a deep breath. "Have you ever heard of Attention Deficit Hyperactivity Disorder?"

"ADHD? Sure, little kids who can't sit still."

"Sort of," Trent agreed. "It's a brain chemistry thing where a person can't concentrate for very long. Sometimes he doesn't think before he does something. Sound like anyone you know?"

Adam raised his eyebrows. "No way! That would explain some of the crazy things you've come up with."

"It's the cold, hard truth! I'm a card-carrying, drug-chugging, ADHD eighteen-year-old," Trent said matter-of-factly. "I can't believe no one suspected it before. It seems everyone thought it was simple bad-assness."

"You said you're taking drugs? What kind?" Adam was intrigued now.

"I'm on *Methylphenidate*, for one. It's an amphetamine known as Ritalin. It really takes the edge off." Trent tossed the pillow he'd been playing with onto an adjacent chair and began explaining the chemical attributes of Ritalin. It quickly got way too technical for Adam, but one word had caught his attention.

"Did you say Ritalin is an amphetamine? Isn't

that speed? How does speed calm a kid down?"

"It's the craziest thing, Adam. In ADHD kids, it does the opposite of what you'd expect. It slows me down, makes me more manageable, just the way dear old dad likes it." His voice had a bitter edge to it. "The tutor he hired specialized in 'high needs' kids like me."

Adam chewed some chips thoughtfully. There had been times when his friend had freaked him out, but if that wild side could be controlled with medication it would be great. "This is huge, Trent. Man, I feel like crap now. You were going through all this and I had no idea. On top of that, you had to recover from the accident." The minute he said it, Adam wished he could take the words back.

"You couldn't have done anything." Trent shrugged. "Don't beat yourself up. My old man's got enough blame to spread around for everyone."

So Trent still wasn't getting along with his hard-liner dad. The only time Adam could remember Trent's dad cutting his son any slack was when he'd been teaching the boys how to road rally.

"Hey, is your dad still into performance rallying in a big way?" Adam asked. "He always had the newest, fastest cars and was really great about letting us hang around. In fact, the first time I drove after getting my learner's licence, I was with your dad in his rally car. He said it was never too early to start."

Trent scoffed, "Yeah. He still thinks he can win the World Rally Championship. And with him, money is no object." He crushed his pop can in his fist. "I remember how he'd let us hang around the garage when he and his friends worked on their cars, but only if we cleaned up the place after they were done."

Adam smiled. "I didn't mind cleaning up. I learned a lot from watching those guys twist wrenches, and eavesdropping on the drivers was cool. I think your dad wanted you to hang around, but didn't want to come off looking like a softy. So he found a way for you to do it legally … with a broom!"

Rallying had been the dream Adam and Trent shared. They'd practised their driving skills every chance they got and, once they had more experience under their belts, the boys had planned on entering the Western Canada Rally Championship. But all that was before the accident. Trent didn't look in shape to drive and, as for Adam, he hadn't sat behind the wheel of a rally car since, well, *that* night.

Rally driving had been his passion and he'd been good at it, but things were different now. He took a long swallow of his pop.

Trent rubbed his eyes as though he were immensely tired. "It seems like a million years ago." He moved his bad leg off the stool. "So, are you still fired up about rallying? Did you get to see the Paris–Dakkar when you were over there? Did you enter any desert rallies when you were in Saudi Arabia?" Now bubbling with excitement,

Trent rapid-fired his questions.

"Ah, actually, no." Adam avoided looking at his friend's face. "We lived in a special compound and you couldn't go anywhere without permission, let alone drive like a wild man in the desert. If we'd stayed, I planned to go to the United Arab Emirates Desert Challenge in Dubai, but that wasn't until October."

"Then we'd better get you back in the game," Trent said eagerly. "Hey, you won't stay seventeen forever, and champion drivers are made before they hit twenty."

Adam could hear the excitement in Trent's voice. He wondered if the Ritalin would keep Trent's enthusiasm from red-lining, the way it always had done before.

"There's a rally this weekend in the mountains near Banff and the old man is entered. He bought a new Subaru WRX STi and a top shop prepped it. It should be a lot of fun and we can both get our hands back into the world's best sport. It's only about an hour and a half from Calgary. What do you say? It'll be a blast!" Suddenly finding something interesting about the pattern in the carpet, Trent stared at the floor. "I know I used to be a bit of an ass, but it would mean a lot to me." Adam could hear the almost desperate need in Trent's voice. "We'd be like every other kid out there — into the cars and the driving and not worrying about anything else."

Adam searched his mind for an excuse. Before,

he would have loved to go, but now the thought of being with Trent and getting that close to a rally car brought all the nightmares slithering back. "I'm not sure I can make it. We haven't totally unpacked yet and…" He could feel the sweat on his forehead, and his heart had picked up revs.

Zoë smiled warmly at him. "You have to come, Adam. I'm kind of new at the rally stuff and I won't have anyone to talk to if you don't. Besides, once Trent gets near that STi, he really zones out."

Adam tried not to stare at her. It struck him that her shiny cap of auburn hair made her startling emerald-green eyes look enormous. Zoë had changed in the last few months. She seemed a lot more grown up. "Ah … well," he stammered, unable to think.

"Then it's all settled," Zoë interrupted. "Trent will pick you up bright and early Saturday and we'll all go out to the forestry reserve together!"

"No way!" Adam's voice came out much louder than he'd meant.

Both Trent and Zoë stopped, surprised at the volume of his outburst.

"I mean…" He hesitated as he looked at Trent's disfigured face, then saw the hope sparkling in his friend's pale eyes. He knew he couldn't bail again. He'd come this far; he couldn't back out now.

Adam fought past the demons in his mind and tried to smile. "Count me in!"

Chapter 2

"There's nothing like springtime in the Rockies."
Zoë shivered as she zipped up her coat against the
chilly Banff morning. They stood high on a
thickly forested hill. All around them, the craggy
grey mountains crowded in like eager fans on race
day.

Adam watched the snow swirling down out of
clouds the colour of charcoal. He'd ridden up on
his motorbike, a red and white CBR 600, and was
still trying to thaw out. "You're right. This is nothing like springtime … *anywhere*."

When Adam had told his parents he was hanging out with Trent again, they'd had mixed
feelings. His mom had been skeptical because of
the past trouble Trent had been in, and Adam
could understand that. His dad, as usual, had tried
to be fair. "I want you to be able to put the past to
rest, son, and I'm glad everything's okay between
you and Trent. But please keep in mind that he has

a tendency to be a little offside in the things he does. In fact, before the accident, your mother and I were concerned about the direction you were headed."

After Adam explained about the ADHD, his parents had been more understanding, but still had reservations. He'd assured them Trent was a different guy on medication. Now, looking at his friend, he hoped he hadn't been mistaken.

Trent rubbed his hands together vigorously and blew on his fingers. "No worries. The snow will burn off by ten o'clock, and it will make for super sloppy racing." Their hilltop perch overlooked the service area where the rally cars were worked on before the start of each special stage, when the actual racing happened. Trent turned in a three-sixty. "From this spot, we can see both the first and second special stages! You have to hand it to Shawn Bishop and the boys at the Calgary Sports Car Club, they don't forget about spectators when they set these things up." He ran his hand through his sandy brown hair.

Adam noticed Trent's hair was combed so it covered his misshapen ear, and he felt for his friend. He could understand Trent wanting to get back into racing, where what counted was being the fastest driver on the course, not what you looked like.

Adam had seen pictures of Formula One superstars Niki Lauda and Alex Zanardi, who'd been badly disfigured in crashes but returned to win and become heroes at the sport they loved. When someone thought of Niki Lauda, all that came to mind was a man who could lap consistently faster than any other driver out there, not the fact he'd been terribly burned.

Suddenly, Adam felt another load of guilt added to the weight that pressed down on him. Despite Trent's boast about being busy with the ladies, Adam suspected his friend had been exaggerating a little or, more likely, a lot. There hadn't been a mention of a girlfriend, past or present, and no one called him on his cell phone. No wonder Trent was so fired up about getting back here, back to where people saw past his broken outside to the brilliant young driver that was waiting inside.

Adam gazed at the mountain slopes surrounding them, and the mix of evergreen and deciduous trees crowding up to the tree line. "It's almost May, but from those bare birches, you'd think it was November." A sudden gust of wind made the corn snow dance and eddy around them. He shivered involuntarily. "Or December."

Trent didn't seem to mind the brisk air. "Not important. It won't affect the driving. In half an hour this course will be hot." He waved down the hill to where his dad's new Subaru was parked amid two dozen cars of various makes, models, and vintages. "Come on, let's find out why the old man's STi is so much better than all these others."

"I brought dad's mini-camcorder to record his first rally in the new car. He'll think it's cool that

27

I taped it!" Zoë pulled an incredibly small video device out of her jacket. "This is so exciting!" She peered through the viewfinder, panning across the parked cars below, and began speaking to the machine. "I'm your host, Miss Zoë Kendall, and this is a video record of my dad's first flight in the new STi."

"Put that thing away, Zoë," Trent admonished. "We've got some serious checking out to do."

They started down the steep hill. The light dusting of snow made the shale scree slippery and the footing dangerous.

"Zoë, you'd better go in the middle in case you spaz out and take a header." Trent nudged his sister protectively between Adam and himself, then started slowly hobbling down the hill ahead of her, his damaged leg dragging a little.

Zoë eyed Trent's leg and Adam thought she was going to make a comment, but instead, she put one hand on her brother's shoulder. "Lead on, but if I end up on my toque, I'm taking you with me! I'll need something soft and squishy to land on."

Adam followed, making sure he was close enough to Zoë to grab her in case she fell. He didn't want to see either of them hurt.

*　*　*

As they drew closer to the cars, the rhythmic metallic rasp of ratcheting wrenches made Adam smile, and the sound of the engines warming up had his pulse racing. Everywhere drivers, co-drivers, and support crew bustled about in the organized chaos that always preceded a rally. He'd missed this.

"Did you add the ferro-carbon pads to the Brembos or not? I don't want any brake fade," Steven Kendall barked at his mechanic as they walked up.

"I see you're still working on your people skills." Trent edged past his father to peer under the raised hood of the bright blue car.

His dad whirled on him. "About time. You said you'd be here to help set up our service area." He stopped when he saw Adam. "Adam Harlow, well I'll be. I haven't seen you since," he furrowed his brow. "Since the accident. Are you driving in the rally today?"

The man's tone was brusque and Adam cleared his throat awkwardly. He wondered if Mr. Kendall was ticked at him for trashing his car. "No, sir. I'm just here to support Team Kendall." He tilted his head at the STi. "Nice ride."

Mr. Kendall's tone became more relaxed. "It should do the job." He glanced at his mechanic. "If Jorge has done his."

The mechanic shook his head good-naturedly, smiling as he finished wiping a spotless wrench with a rag. "Don't worry, Steven. This car has serious heat," he said in heavily accented English.

"I wouldn't mind trying this buggy out some-time. It looks sweet." Trent ran his hands along the gleaming fender of the car.

"Do you think you're up to it?" His father gave him a calculating look. "If that Ritalin is working, you should be a lot smoother driver than you used to be."

Adam could almost see Trent flinch.

"I guess the only way to find out for sure is to let me drive." Trent stood his ground and stared coolly back at his dad. A tense look ricocheted between Trent and his father.

Before their tempers could flare, Zoë insinuated herself between the two. "I'd like a chance to drive too, Dad. I've been going over every set of pace notes I could find, and Jorge has been teaching me about weight transfer, torque, and all kinds of tech stuff."

The senior Kendall refocused his attention on his daughter. "You, drive? You don't have your licence to drive in a rally, let alone the experience needed."

Zoë put her hands on her hips. "I'm sixteen and I've had my licence for three months."

"Easy now, honey." Mr. Kendall put his arm around her shoulders. "I'm talking about the special licence issued by C.A.R.S. so that you can drive in competition. You have to have your regional licence to begin rallying."

"What's stupid C.A.R.S.?" she asked, her lips forming a classic pout.

"You've got it backward, Zoë," Trent teased. "It's the Canadian Association of Rally Sport, *stupid!*"

Zoë glared at her brother, then sighed. "I suppose

Trent has his special licence and I bet *you* helped him practise for it, Dad."

"Hey, I'm the first-born son, little sister," Trent smirked at her.

"Right, I forgot. The male heir to the throne," she retorted sarcastically.

"Speaking of driving…" Trent broke in. "Since you have the STi, that frees up the Lancer Evo 4 that you drove last year. It would be awful for a car that fast to sit in the garage during rally season."

Rubbing his chin, Mr. Kendall looked from the STi to Trent. Adam wondered if he was going to offer the Evo to his son to drive. He knew that it would make Trent extremely happy. "Trent, I'm still not convinced you have that ADHD totally under control. I don't want to see you wrapping the Evo around the first tree that gets in the way. But maybe if you were co-driver with someone more level-headed. You know, avoiding problems is the key to good rallying."

Adam saw Trent's expression harden. He barely noticed that Mr. Kendall had turned his attention from his son to him.

"Adam," he went on, "If I remember correctly, before the accident you were shaping up to be a pretty fair driver. I believe in giving people *one* second chance." His eyes narrowed as he scrutinized Adam. "There are rallies scheduled in the next few weeks. Do you think you could handle the Evo, with Trent as your co-driver?"

Adam's face flushed. "Actually, sir, I haven't

been doing any rallying. I'm sure Trent would make a far better driver." A bead of sweat trickled slowly down his back like a drop of hot lead.

"I'll get my regional licence and I could be his co-driver!" Zoë volunteered brightly.

"No way, Zoë," said Trent, breaking his stony silence. "Adam's going to be my partner; just like we planned years ago when we ice raced. Right, Adam?"

Adam remembered frosty Saturdays sliding cars around on frozen lakes, bumping and bashing to win. You learn a lot about skid control when there's nothing for your tires to grab onto. Adam heard the note of desperation in Trent's voice and knew he needed support.

"Right! I can navigate, no problem. I just need to brush up on decoding the pace notes." When he and Trent had switched from ice racing to rallying, Adam had been the co-driver, the navigator, who used the detailed list of corners and obstacles to tell the driver what to expect next on the twisty course. The co-driver read what was coming and the driver responded with absolute faith the right-hand turn they were going into would then veer left just as he'd been told. A good co-driver was the edge between winning and wishing.

Trent's dad seemed pleased. "Then it's settled. Talk to Jorge about practice tomorrow at the cabin. This might be just what's needed to straighten you out, Trent." He checked his watch and started toward the STi. "Time to find my co-driver. Enjoy the day.

I'll see you at the red board, final stage. Oh and Trent — about tomorrow … don't break the car."

Mr. Kendall spoke in a light tone, but Adam saw Trent's lips tighten as he nodded curtly, acknowledging his dad's parting order. In addition to the anger, Adam caught a glimpse of something else in Trent's eyes. He saw his friend's seriously hurt feelings.

Chapter 3

As he waited for the rally to begin, Adam thought about practising the next day. An image of himself and Trent strapped into the Evo leaped into his mind, and his hands started to shake. He quickly stuck them into his pockets. Maybe if he navigated and didn't actually drive, this sick feeling would go away. He had faith in Trent's driving, but that didn't help the lump in his throat. It was the idea of sitting next to his disfigured friend in a car with a roll cage that choked Adam, squeezing the air out of his lungs until he felt he would never breathe again.

Adam knew he wouldn't be able to come up with a way out. There was no reason he and Trent couldn't be side by side in that car tomorrow. The Evo was a sweet ride and they both had all the qualifications needed to be in it.

Rallying didn't depend on having the fastest car or being a certain age. If you were old enough to hold a valid driver's licence and had attended a performance driving school, you could tune up nearly any set of wheels and put it in a rally. That was the beauty of the sport — it was accessible to everyone and didn't depend on a limitless bank account. Of course, if you had big bucks to throw at your car, you could prep it better and increase your chances of a win, but for most rallyers, it was the thrill of driving that had them hooked.

"Hey, is that Marcus Dreger?" Zoë asked excitedly as she scanned the crowd. "He is *so* hot. He's practically a god at school."

Adam followed her gaze to the tall, athletic blond zipping up his fireproof Nomex driver's suit. Marcus looked over and waved, then started toward them.

"Forget about this guy, Zoë," Trent advised. "He's bad news."

Zoë ignored her brother. "He's doing super this year. They say at eighteen, he may be the youngest driver to get offered a position with a professional team."

Adam watched Marcus come closer. Zoë smoothed an errant strand of her sleek hair back behind her ear and smiled in a way that made Adam wish she were looking at him.

"Trent, old buddy, great day for a fast drive." Marcus tucked his flashy helmet under his arm and turned to Adam. "Hey, Harlow. Long time, no see. I heard you were in some crazy hot country with a lot of sand and it wasn't Saskatchewan."

He laughed at his own joke. "What happened, did a resident oil sheik decide you foreign devils had to vacate the premises?"

Adam didn't feel like explaining. "Something like that."

Zoë cleared her throat and Marcus turned, his eyebrows going up in surprise. "Who are you, and what are you doing wasting your time with this loser?" He flashed her a wide smile as he tipped his head in Trent's direction.

"She's my sister, so back off, Marcus." Trent's voice had a hard edge.

Zoë glared at her brother, then turned to Marcus. "I'm Zoë and I love a man in a uniform." She giggled as she glanced appreciatively at Marcus's snug driving suit, which showed off his athletic build.

"Always like to dress for success." Marcus moved a little closer.

"You can forget it, Dreger. She's out of your league." Trent took a protective step toward his sister. "Don't you have a rally to drive?"

"Actually, I have a rally to *win*. I don't want to keep my fans waiting, which means I'd better find my co-driver so we can make some magic happen." Marcus winked at Zoë. "See you again soon." He turned and strode back to his car.

"He is such a first-class loser," Trent commented sourly. "And Gary Towes is his co-driver. Towes isn't even in school and he's a lot older than Marcus. I've been hearing stuff about him for years, and not all of it good. Not the kind of guy you'd think a cop's kid would hang with. As for that car of Marcus's ... I heard his police detective dad paid over five big ones for the paint job alone."

Adam thought Marcus's tricked-out black Eagle Talon with its ornate paint and alloy wheels seemed more like a car show model than a rally car, but maybe it had go as well as show.

Zoë whirled on her brother. "You're such a jerk, Trent!" She stamped her foot and stalked away.

"Sisters!" Trent said, watching her retreating back with astonishment. "Go figure."

"I take it that Superjock still goes to Springbank?" Adam asked. "Man, he owned the track team bragging rights. Remember that big provincial meet last year when Marcus showed up with his dad in a squad car with the lights whirling and sirens wailing?" He shook his head. "After he won enough events to make our school a legend, Marcus took everyone out for a victory meal. You and Marcus used to be pretty tight. Do you still hang out?"

"Not much," Trent answered noncommittally. "I have better things to do, and I don't want any of Dreger's action. Another thing I don't want is for Zoë to hang around that loser. And as for driving, Marcus Dreger is a hack." He spun around and started trudging back up to the viewpoint. His awkward gait was painful for Adam to watch.

Adam followed, wondering why Trent would change his opinion of Marcus so drastically. Maybe the accident or the Ritalin had something to do with it. Trent seemed so bitter these days. It reminded Adam of another question he had for his old friend. He caught up to Trent. "Hey, what gives with you and your dad? It was pretty frosty back there."

Trent sighed resignedly. "That's a whole other thing. Because of some stuff I did in the past, the old man thinks I'm a royal screw up, that I can't be trusted to do the right thing."

"But why?" Adam asked.

Trent stopped. "You really want to know?" he asked.

"Yeah, I do," Adam said seriously.

"I guess it started a few years back when I got into a little trouble, the usual — skipping school, graffiti — and once I asked him to help me out of a tough jam, which he never lets me forget about. I don't like to talk about it. It's ancient history, before I knew you."

Adam nodded his head. "It must be strange having a dad who's a wheel in the legal system."

"You don't know the half of it," Trent scoffed. "He plans on retiring from his law firm to go into politics. I think he wants to be king of Canada or something. We all have to stay squeaky clean so we'll look like the perfect little family. That's why he's hoping I've been straightened out chemically." He reached down, picked up a rock, and threw it as hard as he could at a stand of skeletal poplars. "You know what his first words to me were after the accident?"

Adam shook his head.

"He was really flipping out. But it wasn't about the totalled car, or that we could have been killed. The big thing was that we both could have ended up with criminal records for car theft. He told me the only reason that didn't happen was because he couldn't let you burn for something I did, and so he told the cops that we borrowed the car with his permission."

Trent resumed his slow progress up the steep hill, then stopped and leaned heavily against the trunk of an old tree, resting his leg. "I always knew he liked you, Adam, and I was cool with that. He said you were a good influence on me. If it had been only me, I bet he would have pressed charges." Trent continued walking again, not looking at Adam.

A fresh wave of guilt flooded through Adam. "Trent, your dad must have been pretty shook up. But he wouldn't have pressed charges against his own son! Besides, I was driving, not you."

"Yeah, but my old man knows it was my idea to take it in the first place. He says it was a 'logical escalation in my criminal behaviour.' What kind of crap is that to say to your kid? Then on top of that, I turned up with ADHD. You'd have thought I did it on purpose from the way the old man went on."

"You think he blamed you for having ADHD?"

Adam couldn't imagine his own father reacting that way if he'd been diagnosed with a serious medical condition.

"He said it was another problem we would have to work on." Trent laughed mirthlessly. "*We* work on it in the usual way. He opens his wallet and I'm the one doing all the sweating. I bet I saw more specialists than any ADHD kid in history. I did a million tests and was a guinea pig for any drug out there that might make me close to normal."

"Your dad is tough, but it sounds like he was trying to help."

Trent didn't say anything. Instead, he checked his watch and abruptly changed the subject. "Won't be long now. Rally city!"

Adam didn't push it, but he knew the old Trent. His friend had had a way of making trouble happen around him on a continual basis. It would be hard for any parent to stay on a kid's side if the kid kept messing up. Maybe Trent had a short memory — or a faulty one — when it came to his history with his father.

The two boys settled at the vantage spot they'd chosen to watch the competitors make their tortuous way through the carefully laid-out course. Adam could hardly wait to see them come blasting past. It was exciting to watch the drivers push their cars at breakneck speeds down forested roads with tight turns, washouts, and blind corners. The driving skills required were awesome.

Every competitor was given an exact time to

leave the start of each special stage, with one-minute intervals between competitors. Their times were recorded when they arrived at the finish, muddy or dusty and sometimes battered, with the fastest team being the winner of that section. The team with the least accumulated time for all the special stages determined the final winner.

"It's all about weight transfer," Trent muttered as he watched through the binoculars they'd brought. His father's STi expertly manoeuvred several tight hairpins in a series of perfectly controlled skids.

The car would start out in a slide one way, then the driver would tap the brakes, crank the wheel, and pour on the power to make it swing like a pendulum around the tight corner. The mud flew in every direction as the STi was put through its paces.

"That, and left foot braking," Adam added, peering through his own field glasses and feeling better than he had in a long time. He loved this sport. He and rallying were a natural fit.

Trent swivelled his binoculars. "Man, the section of road they're coming to looks like moguls on a ski hill. This should be good."

Lowering his glasses for a moment, Adam watched Trent. He was excited, but not wild like he'd been in the old days. Adam had noticed subtle changes in his friend and wondered if it was the Ritalin or simply that the accident had made Trent grow up.

The STi caught air on the second hill, the slightly soft suspension nearly bottoming out when the agile car connected with the ground again.

"Ouch! That's got to hurt!" Trent winced as he watched the car continue to take a pounding as it was driven at the edge of control.

"That was full droop for sure. What's your dad use for protection?" Adam asked.

Trent's lips twitched mischievously. "I don't think Mom worries about that anymore."

Adam grimaced at his friend's dumb joke. "Under the car, Doofus, the *skid plate* under the car."

"Oh, *that* kind of protection. It used to be high-density polyethylene; now it's aircraft aluminum with carbon fibre for the sump."

Adam whistled. "Big bucks."

"Yeah," Trent agreed. "The old man doesn't flinch at high-priced extras. He likes to win."

They watched the rest of the cars speed through the first two stages, then decided to head back down the hill to the service area to grab some food from the Kendalls' cooler. Trent assured Adam it would be stocked with more than enough to feed them all.

They had just finished eating when Adam spotted Zoë walking toward them. He handed her a sandwich, which she devoured hungrily.

"I decided to stay down here with Marcus's crew and cheer him on, maybe pick up a few pointers, but he broke the front axle and DNF'd on the third stage." She reached into the cooler for a soft drink. "That 'Did Not Finish' sucks. He was doing great. Marcus caught a ride back with the sweep vehicle. They'll tow his Talon in later."

"It doesn't matter." Trent shook his head as he grabbed a handful of brownies. "No one will touch the old man's STi. We watched him drive the first two stages and he's incredible, a real rocket!"

They made their way to the area where the sixth and final stage would be run, and waited for the cars to pass the red finish board. The total time would determine the ultimate winner, but Adam had to agree with Trent — Mr. Kendall and his bullet STi were a sure win. Adam liked that, despite the problems Trent had with his dad, he still appreciated the great drive his father had today. Mr. Kendall had rocked.

Adam, Trent, and Zoë waited patiently for the marshal's signal that the cars were coming. Adam felt perfectly at home with the enthusiastic fans as he listened to the talk about engines, rallying and who thought which driver handled his car the best and why. The murmur of voices washed over him like a welcome tide. As he eavesdropped, one name kept being repeated as the favourite to win. The fans knew Team Kendall was a lock.

The shrill blast of the marshal's whistle had everyone scrambling out of the way. The first and fastest car, the bright blue STi, blew by them in a scatter of gravel and a cloud of dust. The cheer that went up from the crowd made it obvious everyone thought it deserved the win.

Looking across the service area, Adam could see Marcus's broken Talon being loaded onto a trailer. He felt a stab of pity for Marcus. Rallying was like a force of nature. No matter what you did, some things were beyond your control.

Chapter 4

The next day Adam drove his motorcycle to the Kendalls' luxury log cabin. Although the Kendalls lived in Calgary, they kept the isolated retreat for weekend visits. It was on a large acreage in a remote area bordering the Kananaskis Forestry Reserve. Adam had tried to think of an excuse to get out of the day's planned activities. He'd been there a couple of times before, when he and Trent would watch movies about racing or spend hours discussing what they'd get for a rally car and how they'd prep it. By the time they were finished, the imaginary car would end up costing them a hundred thousand dollars. Adam would laugh and say that's why they still hadn't bought one — they had to wait to win the lottery or discover diamonds in the backyard first.

Trent came out of the house as Adam parked his bike. Together, they walked to the four-car garage where Jorge was working on the canary-yellow Evo.

"Is she ready to go?" Trent asked enthusiastically. "'Cause I know I am."

Jorge smiled. "Your dad says to stay on the property where there are no unexpected surprises, like oncoming traffic. This is your first time back in a car. I think you should take it slowly, at least until you get to the bottom of the driveway."

Trent hooted with laughter. "That's *two* kilometres *too* long *to* wait, Jorge," he said, emphasizing each similar-sounding word.

Trent had told Adam that Jorge thought English was the most confusing language he'd ever heard, and the good-natured mechanic spoke six languages.

"Come on, Adam. Let's find you a helmet." Trent strode to a cabinet containing Nomex driving suits, Peltor helmets with intercoms, gloves, and even spare sunglasses.

"Wow!" Adam gaped at the array of equipment. "Nothing like being prepared."

"The old man keeps it stocked because we test cars here. We have kilometres of roads crisscrossing our property and it makes for some wild rides." Trent handed Adam a helmet, grabbed one for himself, and headed back to the car.

As Adam slowly followed, he tried to keep his stomach from ejecting his breakfast all over the immaculately groomed lawn. The closer he got to the car, the louder the pounding in his ears. Finally, he stood in front of the car. It took everything he had to stop from turning around and bolting for his bike. He fumbled with his helmet, the sweat on his palms making his hands slippery.

It was too late; there was no way he could get out of this now.

With trembling fingers he reached for the door handle, telling himself it was okay, he wasn't driving this car. The accident was in the past. He could do it. He'd just sit quietly beside Trent. They'd go for a quick blast and it would be over.

But as he climbed into the car, claustrophobia clawed at him like a hungry demon. He was sure the steel roll cage was going to squeeze him to death, and his hands shook as he did up his safety harness. As he tried to settle himself in the seat, Adam noticed Trent carefully placing his bad leg in a position that would let him use the floor pedals.

"D-d-does the leg hurt?" he stammered before he could stop himself.

Trent buckled up. "Naw, twinges mostly. It's the lack of flexibility that really ticks me off. I go to physiotherapy every week, but it's not helping. I guess I'm stuck with it."

Adam thought of the years stretching ahead with Trent's leg getting no better.

"We'll just get a feel for it again before we open her up." Trent grinned mischievously and Adam hoped his friend's medication was working. Trent could be a particularly spinny driver when he was wound up, and spinny was not a good thing behind the wheel of a powerful car.

Adam heard his own ragged breathing as he

turned on his helmet intercom. "Can you hear me?" he rasped.

"Loud and clear." Trent gave Adam a questioning look. "Hey, you sound a little nervous, old buddy. You're not still shook up from the accident, are you?"

Adam's heart jumped into his throat. Trent knew! But when he looked at his friend's concerned face, he saw Trent didn't have it in him to torture Adam this way. Trent trusted Adam in the car with him, and Adam had to at least pretend to do the same. He shook his head and tried to sound cool. "No way, man!"

"Then this is going to be great. Hang on!" Trent punched the car into first gear and they shot off down the long curving drive.

"Whoa! I thought we were going to get our sea legs back before dialling this thing up." Adam knew his voice was shaking, but so was the rest of him.

"Don't be such a chicken. I know this road like the back of my hand!" Trent blasted through the gears and the nimble car responded instantly. The road flashed by under them as they flew past the tall pine trees at a dizzying pace.

The sweat began pouring down Adam's face. Before they'd reached the bottom of the long driveway, his stomach started heaving. "Pull over, Trent. I'm going to puke."

Trent glanced at Adam, who must have looked pretty rough, because Trent pounded on the brakes. A cloud of dust enveloped the car.

Adam stabbed the release on his belts and clambered out just as his breakfast decided to leave. His stomach twisted as he wretched again. Finally, the spasm was over, and Adam thanked the racing gods he was wearing an open-faced helmet. He wiped his mouth with the back of his hand.

"I've never seen you carsick before. What's the matter?" Trent lowered his voice. "Hey, old buddy, this doesn't have anything to do with the accident does it? You know, like weird flashbacks or something?"

Adam couldn't believe Trent had hit so close to the mark. Had he been that transparent? He heard the concern in his friend's voice and scrambled for some way to throw him off. Adam turned his face from his friend and from the truth. "I'm okay. I must have eaten something bad for breakfast." He desperately wished he'd never agreed to this. Being in a car with Trent was too much for him. Then, seeing the worry on Trent's face, he shook his head. "Don't worry. I'm fine. I'll just walk back to clear my head."

"Maybe you need to take a Gravol before flying with me!" Trent quipped as he studied Adam. "You sure you're okay, man?"

Adam smiled sheepishly. "Don't worry about me. I'll be fine. You take this buggy out for a blast and I'll meet you at the cabin."

Climbing the hill, Adam could hear the sound

of Trent smoking through the gears. He couldn't believe he'd tossed his breakfast! He and cars had always been the best of friends, but after today, he couldn't say that any longer. He'd never wanted to get away from a car so badly in his whole life.

Just as Adam reached the top of the long driveway, Trent roared past in the Evo. He parked the car and, grinning from ear to ear, waited for Adam. "Glad to see you made it. What a hoot!" Trent slapped him on the back as they started for the house.

Adam shot him a dark look, but didn't say anything. He still felt lousy.

"Hey, I tried to watch you guys, but you flashed by so quickly I couldn't keep up! You two were flat-out fast." Zoë, sitting with one leg dangling over the arm of her deck chair, smiled at them as they rounded the corner of the wide veranda. "I couldn't see clearly because of the trees, but I thought you stopped at the bottom of the hill. What happened?" she asked, looking from Trent to Adam.

Trent raised an eyebrow at his sister. "Zoë, when you get a little older, you'll learn not to ask a guy, or a bear, what he does in the woods." Laughing, he punched Adam on the shoulder. "Come on, we earned a cold drink."

As they started into the house, Adam was grateful to Trent for not teasing him or telling Zoë that he'd not only thrown up his last meal, but had walked back. It would mean a round of questions, and he didn't want Zoë to have any hint that he was terrified to ride in a car with her brother.

Adam wondered what would happen the next time he strapped himself into the Evo. From the way Trent was practically bouncing off the ceiling, Adam knew there would definitely be a next time.

Chapter 5

Adam climbed the worn school steps and waited as Trent laboriously followed with his weird, hopping gait. The weathered brown sandstone building was old and solid, but built before they worried about such niceties as wheelchair ramps or elevators for the disabled. Trent's limited flexibility was enough to deal with the clutch, brake, and accelerator pedals in a car, but wouldn't let him walk normally or handle obstacles like stairs very easily.

Feeling like a little kid on his first day of school, Adam nervously held the door open for Trent. "Man, it feels strange to be back here." He had to remind himself that it had only been a few months and not the lifetime it seemed since he and Trent had walked together down these musty halls.

"Its charm will wear off quickly, trust me." Trent moved down the crowded hallway flanked with battered green lockers. "You can share a locker with me. This late in the year, there won't be any free," he said, opening the dented metal door.

In addition to the usual assortment of very ripe gym clothes, hardly used textbooks, and lunch bag cast-offs, Adam noticed the large bottle of pills sitting on the top shelf.

Trent caught him staring. "I have to take my Ritalin every three hours, so I leave it here. Don't freak on me; the school narcs know."

Adam inspected the myriad pictures pasted onto the inside of the door. Some shots showed cars airborne, all four tires off the ground; others had well-known rally drivers, their faces wreathed in victorious smiles. There was also a snapshot of Adam and Trent holding up their certificates from performance driving school the previous year. Adam remembered that day. It had been one of the best of his life. He noticed a scrap of paper with a scribbled phone number taped beside a picture of an Eagle Talon. "Secret girlfriend?" he asked, tilting his head at the number.

"No, it's Marcus Dreger's cell." Trent finished clearing some of his junk from the bottom shelf. "He gave it to me last fall when we were hanging out. It's garbage now." In one swift movement, he ripped the number off the door and crumpled it in his fist.

Adam unloaded his books and binders, then they stowed their coats.

"Man, I'd say this thing is stacked and packed to the max." Trent laughed, inspecting the over-stuffed locker.

Just then, Marcus Dreger strolled up. He was dressed as if he'd fallen out of a Gap ad. Adam could feel the confidence he exuded. This was his turf and he knew it.

"Well, how about this. Trent's got a new roomie." He glanced slyly at Adam. "You his new mule?"

Adam was confused by Marcus's question, and looked to Trent for an explanation.

"Shut your mouth, Dreger," Trent growled.

"Is that any way to talk to an old friend? Come on, Trent, loosen up." He glanced at the pill bottle, still bearing the plastic seal. "You've restocked the pharmacy, I see." He reached for it, but Trent slammed the door closed before he could grab it.

"We've got to get to class, Marcus." Trent slung his backpack over his shoulder and started to leave, then turned and added, "Hey, too bad about the DNF. That really sucks. It would have been cool to see someone beat the old man, even you."

Marcus's demeanour changed with the subject and his face clouded. "Yeah, that was totally bogus." His tone was sharp and bitter. "I'm not worried; I'll get him next time. My dad says it had to be a faulty axle. I told him it sure wasn't my driving. I had that stage nailed."

Adam knew mechanical failures were all part

of rallying and was surprised that Marcus would make such a big deal about it.

Marcus went on without pausing. "Hey, speaking of your family, where have you been hiding that sister of yours, Trent? She's one fine little piece of—"

Adam cut him off, "I wouldn't finish that thought if I were you."

"Watch your mouth, Dreger!" snarled Trent.

"Can't I pay a lady a compliment?" Marcus asked innocently. "I've got to go. See you later, Trent, same as usual."

Adam watched him walk away and he wondered at Marcus's last comment. Hadn't Trent said he wasn't hanging with Marcus anymore?

The throng of kids in the hall was brutal and Adam, concerned for his friend's leg, tried unsuccessfully to clear a path through the shifting currents of students. Guilt cut through him. The last time they had gone to class together, Trent had been whole, not a damaged invalid.

Ignoring Adam's feeble attempt at crowd control, Trent pushed past him and led the way, unfazed by his handicap. "Hey, we have chemistry with Mr. Price last period this morning," Trent reminded him as they manoeuvred down the congested hallway, "the only bright spot in my dreary day. I love playing god and making things happen in a test tube. I'm working on a special project and Mr. P. is really impressed."

Adam heard the enthusiasm in his voice. Trent

had always been a chemistry star but because of his behaviour problems, which tended to spill over into class, he had never received the recognition he deserved. Trent used to hate school, and Adam was surprised to see him so animated and excited. "Okay, so tell me about it. But please, keep the language at a level I can understand, Einstein."

Trent began describing an extremely complicated experiment, and Adam had trouble following. He made approving noises to show support as Trent babbled on about chemical bonds, ion exchange, and coefficients of friction.

* * *

As both hands on the clock crawled slowly toward the magic twelve position, Adam impatiently waited for the end of their chem class. Finally, the bell rang and he gratefully closed his binder. Looking at his friend, Adam rolled his eyes. "Brutal!"

Trent was even smarter than Adam remembered. He was easily a chemistry genius, whereas Adam could have dropped into the wrong class by mistake. He hadn't realized how far behind he'd fallen. It was a good thing his best friend was such a whiz and could give him some pointers.

"I'm going to stay for a couple of minutes and talk to Mr. P. about my project." Trent pulled a sheaf of papers out of the back of his notebook. "Why don't I meet you in the cafeteria? Zoë said, even though she usually wouldn't be caught dead with her older brother, she wanted to have lunch with us today to celebrate your first day back."

"No problem. See you in ten." Adam grabbed his backpack and rushed out. He'd had enough chemistry talk for one day, and the prospect of lunch with Zoë Kendall was definitely appealing.

The cafeteria was crowded and smelled like boiled meat. Remembering what that distinctive odour meant, Adam decided it must be undercooked-spaghetti-and-rubber-meatball day or maybe greasy-meatloaf-and-lumpy-mashed-potato day. Either way, it meant some gross grey sludge that really stuck in your gut. He spotted Zoë eating a large salad and, grabbing a tray and a plate of spaghetti and meat-balls, made his way to her table.

Her eyes lit up when she saw him. Her wide smile made Adam's neck feel uncomfortably warm.

"How's your first day back at the salt mine?" she asked as soon as he'd sat down.

"You'll be happy to know, it's going great. Trent will be here in a few minutes. He's talking to Mr. Price about some chemistry mumbo jumbo." Adam took a bite of one of the meatballs and grimaced. "Tastes like they added more rub-ber to today's batch. They're even chewier than usual."

Zoë giggled, peering at him from under her long dark lashes. "I think I read somewhere this is where old rally tires go to be recycled," she whispered conspiratorially. She poked one of the meatballs on his plate with her fork before making a twisted face any five-year-old would have been proud of.

Adam found himself smiling at her and couldn't seem to stop.

"Tell me about living in Saudi," Zoë asked with interest. "It must be very cool to live in another culture, and such a different one from ours."

"I wasn't there long enough to get to know much about the culture, but one thing I learned instantly — never get too close to the business end of a camel. Make that either end! Those rotten beasts like nothing better than to spit gallons of the slimiest stuff this side of a toxic waste dump." Adam couldn't seem to tear his eyes away from Zoë's face. He knew he was embarrassing himself, but couldn't stop.

She laughed and Adam found himself laughing with her. He spent the next thirty minutes telling her about his short experience living in a very foreign country. He liked how she listened attentively and got all his jokes. He discovered that he also liked to hear her opinions on things, and found talking with her an easy and thoroughly enjoyable experience.

"This sounds like I'm in kindergarten, but when I grow up, I want to travel." Zoë's eyes shone as she confided in Adam. "I'm going to climb the pyramids in Egypt, tilt at windmills in Holland, waddle with the penguins in Antarctica, and jog on the Great Wall of China."

"All without breaking a sweat … or a nail!" Adam added teasingly.

Zoë punched him playfully on the arm. "I should make you come. I'll need a roadie to carry my bags." She glanced at her watch. "Where do you suppose big brother got to? He's going to miss lunch if he doesn't get here pronto."

Adam hadn't missed Trent one bit, but his conscience prodded him to find out what was keeping his friend. Reluctantly, he stood up. "I'll go check. Maybe he found someplace better to eat than this four-star Squat and Gobble." Returning his empty tray, he started back toward Mr. Price's classroom. Maybe the two science geeks had started discussing molecules and formulas, and lost track of time. Perhaps Trent had run into a friend and had been sidetracked. Adam dismissed this idea immediately. He knew there were a few guys in rallying who tolerated Trent's unpredictable behaviour because he was a good driver, but here at school, it was a different story. No one wanted to be at ground zero when Trent went off.

Adam had just rounded a corner when he stopped abruptly. Trent was standing by his open locker, and he wasn't alone.

Marcus Dreger stood there beside Trent, stuffing something into his backpack. He was wearing a warm-up suit with *Springbank Track and Field* embroidered across the back and the word *Captain* stitched on the sleeve. Adam figured Marcus must have come from a practice. Trent didn't look happy.

Adam walked over, feeling like an eavesdropper or maybe a party crasher. "What's the holdup, Trent? Zoë's been waiting for you in the cafeteria. You're not having a problem, are you?" He stared directly at Marcus as he spoke.

The tall athlete's tanned face took on a condescending look that instantly annoyed Adam. "I'm picking up my *edge*, Harlow," Marcus said with a lazy drawl. "Hasn't Trent filled you in on the score yet?"

"Ah, actually, we were just finishing up. Later, Marcus." Trent closed his locker door and abruptly started toward the cafeteria.

He could move at surprising speed with his hobbling gait, and Adam had to hurry to keep up. "I thought you weren't buddies with Dreger any more."

"I'm not." Trent avoided looking at Adam.

"Look, Trent, cut the crap. What Marcus said back there made it sound like you were dealing, and that's what it looked like."

Trent stopped and checked to make sure the hallway was empty. "Are you nuts? I'm not selling drugs to Marcus. Adam, everything's cool. I was giving him back some junk of his I found at home, you know, from before."

Adam knew he meant from before the accident and instantly backed off — that was one dark topic he didn't want to get into. He wanted to believe his friend. Maybe he had misinterpreted what he saw and heard.

* * *

Last class that afternoon was English. Adam was sitting beside Trent when the teacher walked in. Ever since he had caught Trent with Marcus, Adam had noticed his friend seemed jumpy and distracted.

The minute the teacher sat at her desk, Trent suddenly slammed his book shut and began talking very loudly to Adam.

"This is crap!" he exploded. "Why do we have to learn about some dead poet from a hundred years ago?" Kids sitting around them turned to stare.

Trent went on. "And this guy isn't even Canadian. You'd think if we have to study some whacked-out poet, it could at least be one from our own country!"

The teacher stood up. "Is there a problem, Trent?"

Trent pulled himself to his feet. "You bet there's a problem. We should be studying Canadian poets, not these dead foreigners." He began agitatedly limping up and down the rows, slamming students' textbooks closed.

Adam was astonished. This was just like the old Trent, the Trent before the Ritalin. Adam wondered if his friend had forgotten to take his medication. He sure wasn't the calm, controlled guy who'd driven so smoothly at breakneck speed yesterday.

"Perhaps we'd better continue this discussion in the office." The teacher moved cautiously toward Trent.

"This isn't a discussion. It's the school board imposing their antiquated ideals about what's great literature on kids who have no choice." He was waving his arms around now. "If you want to hear relevant poetry, try listening to Morissette's *Jagged Little Pill*. Man, that's a classic in any country, and it's home-grown!"

Adam watched Trent and the teacher leave the classroom. It was a little scary how quickly Trent had changed back into the volatile guy he used to know. Maybe he needed his dosage upped.

* * *

Adam waited for Zoë in the coffee shop. He'd spent a couple of days researching ADHD and Ritalin on the Internet and now needed answers, which he hoped Trent's sister could provide.

"Do they have iced lattes at this place?" Zoë asked, tossing her jacket on the back of her chair.

Adam's pulse quickened. She had a way of making him feel like the sun had suddenly broken through the clouds. "I think that can be arranged."

He ordered drinks and, as they waited, he began asking his questions. "Zoë, what happened with Trent? I was there in English class that day, and it was pretty weird."

Zoë rolled her eyes. "The usual. The teachers

and my folks consulted with Trent's doctor, and then they upped his Ritalin again."

Adam's brow furrowed in concentration. "Can you tell me more about the ADHD? How serious is it, what dosage is Trent on now — anything that would help me understand his condition more." He hoped she didn't think his curiosity was ghoulish. He really wanted to understand what was going on with Trent. From what he'd learned from his research, Trent and his wild ADHD weren't exactly a textbook case. Maybe he'd misunderstood what he'd read, but he didn't think so.

"Yeah, sometimes Trent acts nuts. In fact, at times he seems way worse than before he was diagnosed. When he wigs out, the parents go into a flap and haul him off to the witch doctor. He's had his dosage upped three times already." Their drinks arrived and Zoë took a sip. "If you ask me, I think it's one big attention-getting device. Dad is forever hovering over him, and I've heard him and Mom discussing 'poor little Trent and his ADHD.' They're worried he may never finish university or hold down a regular job."

"But I thought he had a relatively mild case. He should be totally under control with his dosage," Adam said, puzzled. This wasn't making sense.

Zoë went on, "Originally it was mild, but the past few months, he's been going downhill fast, lots of problems at school with teachers and acting out at home. I think he's faking it, but if he's not … holy bipolar! My brother is a poster kid for

Mental Mush Week."

Adam stirred a heaping spoon of sugar into his latte. None of this was adding up. "Maybe the docs are missing something. Could it be anything else? Maybe a problem left over from the accident? His head took a real beating." Adam was having a hard time dealing with Trent's physical injuries. The idea that Trent's mental health may also have been affected by the accident was a horrible possibility.

"I don't think so." Zoë scrunched up her face, making the sprinkling of cinnamon freckles across her nose stand out. "He had every test under the sun, but it's Trent. Who knows what evil lurks in the head of my schizy brother." She glanced at her watch. "Oh my gosh! How did it get so late?"

Frantically, she rummaged in her backpack for her cell phone. "Give me a minute." Searching her pockets, she finally pulled a slip of paper out of her jacket. As she tried to read the number, she fumbled the phone and dropped the note.

Adam bent to pick it up.

"No!" She snatched at the paper before Adam could retrieve it from the floor. "I mean, it's okay. I've got it."

Adam caught a quick glimpse of the number before she crumpled the paper. He'd seen it before. Up until that morning, Trent had the same one on his locker door. It was the number of Marcus Dreger's cell phone.

"Butterfingers me!" Zoë giggled nervously as

she dialled and moved out of earshot. She spoke quickly, then snapped the little flip phone shut and returned to the table. "Look, I've got to go." Her face was flushed with excitement. "I promise, if I notice anything weirder than usual with Trent, I'll give you a call."

Adam watched her hurry out of the coffee shop. Both Zoë and her brother were acting weird. And what was their connection with Marcus Dreger?

Chapter 6

The next weekend was the Cochrane Regional Rally. Run out of a small town not far from Calgary, it was a local event that attracted many teams.

Trent had been extremely excited about going and Adam had agreed to meet him. As long as it didn't involve him actually getting into a rally car with Trent, Adam was more than happy to hang out around the fast competitors.

The morning of the rally, Adam was in the garage checking over his bike when his dad walked in.

"You're up early. Everything okay?" Adam heard the concern in his dad's voice and knew he was still worried about the nightmares.

"Don't worry, Dad. I slept like a baby. In fact, the monsters under the bed have eased up lately." As he said this he realized it was true.

"Maybe being back on good old Canadian soil

has done the trick." Mr. Harlow smiled at Adam, then his tone became more serious. "You and Trent are getting along well. How are things between him and his dad? They used to have some issues."

Adam finished checking the tire pressure. "Trent has his own way of looking at things, especially when it comes to his dad." He felt like he had to stick up for his friend. "Mr. Kendall can be a real hard-ass at times."

Adam's dad pursed his lips. "Maybe, but from the way Trent was going off the rails, he needed a hard-ass at times. Adam, for their own protection, kids need boundaries, some more than others. It's like operating with a safety net. It gives them a chance to get a little life experience under their belts before they have to tackle the really serious stuff."

"Yeah, but kids need freedom to make their own choices, right or wrong, or how are we supposed to get life experience to handle the biggies when they show up? Mr. Kendall seemed to climb all over Trent for every little thing." Adam put the tire gauge away in the toolbox.

"Yes, I remember Trent telling you how hard his dad was on him and how he loved to put one over on his old man. Trent's side, the only one you heard, did make it sound like he had it rough." His dad didn't say anymore, but Adam got the message.

He knew that what Trent said about his father

and what Adam saw for himself were often different. He'd always given Trent the benefit of the doubt because they were buddies, and that's what buddies do.

* * *

The ride out to Cochrane was spectacular. The brilliant morning sun rising over the freshly planted fields made the colours seem brighter and more vivid than Adam remembered. He breathed deeply, savouring the tantalizing smells that filtered into his helmet: newly turned earth combined with the tang of the crisp, pristine air. Adam wished the ride could go on forever. He felt like he was in a special galaxy made just for him, as his bike smoothly ate up the kilometres. The sweet spots seemed particularly satisfying as he swooped through the corners, pushing his bike a little harder than usual. He was in the zone and life was good.

The rally site was well marked and Adam had no trouble finding the service area. He pulled up on his bike as the teams were preparing for the start of the race.

The cars gleamed in the sunshine, their bright paint jobs adding to the festive air. Some of the lucky ones sported sponsorship decals, which meant money to buy the expensive trick parts every team dreamed about. These pricey pieces would coax out of their engines the extra horsepower that was critical to getting the winning edge.

Adam noticed some of the crews were still debating which tires to use: a harder compound that would wear better on the rough gravel or the soft, grippier snow and ice tires that risked premature wear on the dry sections. It was an important decision, as races were often won on the choice of tires, and this time of year a driver could expect a little of everything, from slick ice to dry gravel to muddy washouts. Other crews were tinkering with their engines, doing last-minute tweaking, or deciding what shock stiffness to use.

It all made Adam feel like he was where he belonged. He'd loved cars since he was a kid, and had a dream to design cars, very fast cars, when he graduated from university. He'd like to go to Italy, home of the true classics like Ferrari, Lamborghini, and Maserati, and had been secretly trying to learn Italian in his spare time. His dad encouraged Adam by practising his Italian with him, which frequently left both of them laughing at their terrible pronunciation.

At the far end of the service area, apart from the rest of the cars, Adam saw the glossy black Eagle Talon of Marcus Dreger. Trent had said Marcus, an extreme competitor, was not very popular with the other drivers. He'd been known to play dirty.

Looking past the car to the trailer beyond, Adam spotted Trent talking with Marcus. Trent was angry, and they seemed to be arguing. Marcus's expression made it obvious he was ready to explode. Watching, Adam saw Trent thrust a brown paper bag at Marcus. Marcus grabbed the bag and stuffed it into the pocket of the leather jacket he was wearing over his driving suit.

Adam's eyes narrowed. Despite his friend's denials about dealing, he had a bad feeling about what he was seeing. There was more going on here than a simple disagreement and he feared the worst. He had to find out more for himself.

"Hi, Marcus," Adam said, casually strolling over. "Looks like it's going to be a great day for the rally." His hands were fists inside his pockets, and he was ready to use them if he had to. "You guys need help with anything?"

Marcus seemed to make an effort to sound relaxed when he answered. "No, we were having a little discussion about who's the best driver out here today, that's all." He smiled and Adam was reminded of a cobra mesmerizing its prey before it struck. "I'll see you at the finish, Trent. You boys can buy me a congratulatory drink when they hand me the victory trophy. Good to see you back around the circuit, Harlow."

"Sure, Marcus." Adam noticed Trent's face was flushed, making his scar stand out like a fiery rope.

Trent gave Marcus a hard look. "I'm done here. Let's go, Adam." He turned and began moving away in the jerking gait that was so hard for Adam to watch. Not knowing what else to do, Adam followed, unsure of what had just happened.

"Don't forget what we talked about Trent," Marcus called after them. "I sure won't."

Adam followed Trent through the scatter of cars. They walked on in tense silence until Adam couldn't stand it anymore. He had to know what was going on. "Wait a minute." He grabbed his friend's arm, pulling Trent around to face him. "What was that all about? And don't tell me you were returning some old junk!"

"It was nothing!" Trent snapped, yanking his arm out of Adam's grasp. "Marcus thinks because his dad is some big-time cop and he's passable behind the wheel of a car that he can call the shots. I had to set him straight, that's all."

It hadn't appeared that way to Adam. "I want you to be straight with me, Trent. What's going on with you two? If it wasn't drugs, what were you two arguing about?"

Trent hunched his shoulders; his voice was clipped when he answered. "Forget it, will you? I've got everything under control. I'm asking you as a friend, Adam, *drop it*."

Adam knew that when Trent got like this, there was no use badgering him; he would only close down more.

His mood doing a startling one-eighty, Trent straightened up and slapped Adam on the back. "Forget that jerk. I've got something huge to show you." He guided Adam to the Kendall trailer. Jorge was, as usual, working on the STi, while Mr. Kendall went over the pace notes.

Adam stopped. Beside the STi, the bright yellow Evo sat waiting in the early morning light. It had the number 44 on the doors and looked suspiciously ready to rally.

Adam's pulse quickened and his stomach tightened into a knot. "What's this about, Trent?" He walked stiffly over to the car, peered in, and noticed a helmet sitting on each seat.

"Surprise! You and I are driving in our first rally today." Trent waved his hand, silencing Adam's objections. "I know you're overcome with gratitude, but don't worry, you can buy me a steak later." Moving to the back of the Kendall support trailer, he began rummaging in one of the cabinets. He returned with a driving suit, which he handed to Adam.

"It will probably be a little short in the legs, but the rest should fit." He turned to the car, excitement glowing on his face. "Well, what do you think?"

Adam gawked at the car as though it was going to reach up and rip a chunk out of his intestines.

Trent clambered eagerly into the Evo. Adam stopped, then took an unconscious step backward as Trent settled into the driver's seat. Even standing outside the car was enough to make the sweat start. How was he going to get out of this one?

"I … I don't know what to say." Adam tried to swallow, but his mouth was dry.

"You don't have to thank me for entering us. I know it's short notice. We haven't really practised together since before…" Trent's voice trailed off. "For months," he finished. "But I'm sure it will all come back to you. It's like riding a bike."

Adam rummaged through his mind for some reason he couldn't do this. "I ... I ... I haven't seen the pace notes," he stammered. "I'm not ready."

Trent airily waved his objections away. "Don't worry. Zoë has them."

Trent busied himself doing what he called his "pre-flight checklist," making sure everything in the car was on line and running.

Adam walked over to where Zoë and her father were talking. "Good morning, Zoë, Mr. Kendall." He brushed his hand through his short hair. "Zoë, can I talk to you about the pace notes?"

Mr. Kendall smiled at his daughter. "That's what I like to hear. My daughter's name and 'pace notes' in the same sentence. I'm glad you're showing such an interest in rallying, young lady. It makes it a real family hobby." Zoë beamed at her dad. "Now, you go help Adam. I'm going to see if Jorge has finished tuning the STi's fuel computer, then we have to check a detail with the marshals."

Zoë ran through the notes with a fluorescent pink highlighter, accenting important details and features the driver would encounter. "This is going to be a fun ride for you and my brother." She handed Adam the completed sheets. "Watch out for the corner before the bridge. I heard it's off camber."

Adam's hand trembled as he took the papers. His head was starting to pound. "I'm not sure I can do this. I haven't been in a car much lately." He hoped he sounded casual but, with his throat closing up, it was hard to talk.

"You'll be fine. I've gone over the notes and highlighted anything that could possibly give you trouble." She pushed a strand of hair back behind her ear as Trent clambered out of the Evo and walked over to them.

"Jorge and I were up late last night getting the car ready. It should really howl." Trent shaded his eyes, squinting up at the shimmering bowl of blue overhead. "Man, not a cloud in the sky." Unzipping his driving suit, he wiggled the top half off his shoulders, letting it hang loosely around his waist. "It's going to be smoking hot in that car."

Zoë's eyes strayed past Adam to the far end of the service area where Marcus's Talon was parked. "I'll be right back. I'm going to get a drink."

Trent followed her gaze to where Marcus stood talking with his co-driver. His jaw tightened. "I'll go with you. I could use a cold one." Adam saw an annoyed look cross Zoë's face, but she didn't object when her brother joined her.

Adam examined the notes in his hand. Taking a step toward the Evo, he felt his pulse quicken. He knew he had only minutes to ensure he didn't have to get into the car. Hurrying to Jorge's tool-box, he grabbed a pair of wire clippers, then popped the hood on the Evo.

Glancing around, he made sure there was no

sign of Trent or Zoë returning. He didn't want to get caught now.

He pulled the paper clip off the pace notes and straightened an end, then pulled the electronic lead off one of the fuel injectors. Inserting the paper clip into the lead, he pushed on the wire until it popped loose. Carefully, he cut the wire behind the metal connector that transmitted the signal to the injector, then pushed both pieces back into the assembly and replaced it in the engine. The lead appeared untouched but, with a broken internal wire, the injector wouldn't work.

He knew the car would now run so poorly that they would have no choice but to pull out of the rally. He doubted Jorge would be able to figure out how to get the car back up and running in time.

The sound of approaching voices made Adam's head snap up. Praying his sabotage would work, he quickly closed the hood and was replacing the wire clippers in the toolbox as Trent and Zoë walked over to the car.

"Adam, you'd better get changed. We're supposed to be at the main time control in nine minutes." Trent watched as his father drove the STi to the control zone ready to start. "That's the beast to beat."

"Right." Adam grabbed his suit and moved over to the trailer to change, as Trent got behind the wheel. The other cars were lining up now and the sound of their engines was throbbing like the pounding of war drums in his ears.

A vicious burst of cursing issued from the Evo as Trent tried to turn the engine over. "Come on, come on…" He continued to crank the ignition, but the car sullenly refused to fire. Finally it caught, then stumbled and quit.

Adam zipped up his driving suit and walked over to the hood. "Pop it and I'll check if anything's worked loose." Trent released the hood and Adam began wiggling wires and dutifully checking for obvious signs why the car refused to run.

"It sounds like a fuel problem," Trent growled, climbing out of the car and slamming the door shut. "It was running fine earlier this morning. What the hell happened?"

"I've checked everything here." Adam didn't want Trent snooping under the hood. He quickly fiddled with the battery terminals. "Maybe it was a loose clamp. Try it again."

Trent clambered back into the car and turned over the ignition. It started, but the engine sounded terrible. The motor continued to cough and choke.

"You're supposed to leave in two minutes," said Zoë anxiously, checking her watch.

Trent was nearly frantic now. "I don't know where to look. It's in the fuel system, but we could be all day trying to diagnose what's wrong, where." He hit the steering wheel with his fist. "This really sucks." Climbing out of the car, he looked at Adam dejectedly. "I'm sorry, man, but it looks like we'll have to wait till the next one to get our rallying careers back on track. I'll go tell the marshal we're out." Still cursing under his breath, he headed for the main control area.

Adam watched him go, feeling guilty for pulling such a dirty trick on his friend, but knowing it would have been a lot worse if he'd had to get into that car with him.

Zoë gently touched his arm, startling Adam. "Sorry you don't get to race today. If you want, we can watch the rest of the rally together."

Adam smiled at her. Her offer was probably the only thing in the universe that could make him feel better at that moment. "Sounds good. Give me a few minutes to change and I'll meet you at the spectators' area." She squeezed his arm, then walked away.

He closed the hood on the car, noticing the Talon was gone from the far end of the service area.

Adam thought about the altercation he'd seen between Trent and Marcus. Then he remembered the brown paper bag Marcus had stuffed into the pocket of his leather jacket.

Adam saw Trent still busily talking with the officials. Checking to make sure the service area was totally deserted, he decided it was a good time to take a stroll.

Chapter 7

Marcus's Chevy one-ton tow vehicle sat simmering in the hot sun. Peering inside, Adam saw the leather jacket behind the driver's seat on the floor of the extended cab. Glancing furtively around to make sure no one was watching, he yanked the door open and grabbed the coat. The paper bag was still in the pocket.

Adam pulled it out and checked the contents. The bag contained several bottles of pills, and not just any pills. The bottles were filled with Trent's Ritalin. Adam stuffed the bag back into the pocket and returned the jacket to the floor of the truck.

He had to think this through. Why was Trent selling Ritalin to Marcus? Was it for money? Ritalin is an amphetamine and Marcus could easily re-sell it on the street for a profit. There could be another explanation. What if Marcus was keeping the Ritalin for himself? He was still the number-one star athlete on the track team. Maybe that was no accident; maybe he was giving himself a chemical boost to make sure he was the winner. He'd said he was "picking up his edge" at Trent's locker. Everything crowded into Adam's head at once, and it was all ugly.

Trent and Marcus had hung out together before the accident, but they didn't get along at all now. Why would Trent risk breaking the law to sell drugs to Marcus? And how was he able to get enough of the drug to take it himself and sell it to Marcus?

Adam had the strange sensation that he'd walked into a TV cop show. But his gut told him that what he'd seen was real. Trent was selling drugs to Marcus. But the big question remained — why?

He needed more information before he confronted Trent. First he would talk to Zoë. Maybe she would have some insights that would help him figure out what was going on. He finished changing and went to find Trent's sister.

* * *

At a rally, spectators can be found all along the roads that the special stages are run on, which makes it easy to get someone alone if you want to talk to them. Adam headed over to a crowded spectator area where he'd spotted Zoë standing with a group of particularly boisterous fans. He wondered how he was going to casually ask her if she knew her brother was a drug dealer.

Adam manoeuvred through the crowd to stand next to her. "Hey, Zoë, let's go sit in some shade. I'm cooking in this sun."

Her eyebrows went up in mock surprise, then she giggled. "After your stay in Saudi, I'd have thought this heat would be nothing to a desert boy like you!"

They made their way to the lee of an ancient pine and sat in its welcome shade. So far, Trent was nowhere to be seen, and Adam decided he'd better ask his questions before he showed up.

"Trent seemed really upset about the car, but he took it way better than he would have before. You know, before he was put on Ritalin." Adam gave her a sidelong look. "It must have been quite a shock when Trent was diagnosed with ADHD. I mean it had to affect the whole family."

"I guess," Zoë answered noncommittally as she lay back on the soft moss and gazed up into the tangled branches of the gnarled tree. The day was simmering and the heady smell of sun-warmed scrub grass and pungent pine tar made everything seem hazy, like it was wrapped in a warm, fragrant cocoon.

Adam tried a different approach. "I mean, it must have been tough on *you* to have a brother who was so unpredictable. I bet you were relieved when they found a clinical reason why Trent acted the way he did."

This got her attention. "As a matter of fact, it *was* a big relief." She sat up and turned to him, her enormous eyes dark with sudden seriousness. "No one's ever asked how *I* handled this whole thing before. I guess I was glad he wasn't some nutcase who was going to turn into an axe murderer or something." She drew her brows together. "For years, Trent has been the family focus, but usually for bad reasons. I guess having a disorder like ADHD has let him off the hook for some of the stuff he did. He could be really freaky to live with — ups and downs, playing music at all hours, never staying with one thing long enough to finish it. I guess you'd call him extreme."

Adam agreed sympathetically. "He loves driving, that's obvious. It was a mega-surprise to me that we were entered today. I'm sorry he went to all that trouble and then we DNF'd. I mean, I would have loved to have gone out today, but there's always next time." He picked a piece of spear grass and stuck it between his teeth.

"Oh, really?" she asked suspiciously, a note of mischief in her voice. "Answer me straight. You don't have cold feet about co-driving with my lunatic brother, do you?"

As she turned to look at him, Adam noticed the way the red highlights in her hair shimmered in the occasional ray of sunlight filtering through the branches. He feigned total surprise. "Me? Are you crazy? I've loved cars my whole life! It's a sure bet, one way or another, I'll always be connected with cars, and once I make up my mind about something..." He turned to look directly at her.

"…or *someone*, I'm totally focused on the prize." For a long moment, neither of them needed or wanted to say anything.

Adam cleared his throat as he tried to get the conversation back on track. "You said his ADHD was diagnosed as a pretty mild case, right?"

Zoë thought for a moment. "Trent, right … At first, no problem, then a couple of months ago things went downhill and he started having these episodes. That's when they upped the dosage he was on." She leaned back, propping herself on her elbows. "He started at five milligrams once a day, but now he's on ten milligrams three times a day and he's still not always under control."

Adam was surprised. "Okay, but how tough is it to get more of that stuff? What happens if he loses a bottle of pills or something?"

Zoë's gem-coloured eyes looked up at him, and Adam was struck again by how different they were from Trent's.

"Actually, it's one drug that's not easy to get. Ritalin has a triple prescription — one copy goes to the doctor, one to the drugstore, and one to some narcotics department with the government. It's so there's no double doctoring — you know, same kid, two or three physicians, lots of drugs."

Adam thought for a moment. If Trent needed big doses of the drug to stay functioning, how could he chance selling most of it and reverting to the way he was before the Ritalin?

Zoë rubbed her forehead absently. "You know,

it's an odd thing about Ritalin. It only lasts three or four hours, so Trent is always taking the stuff. But sometimes he takes it and he's still goofy, like it wasn't working or something."

A shrill whistle blew, signalling that a rally car was coming and to clear the way. Two seconds later, an Audi Quattro blasted by, sending a cloud of fine dust over the crowd, which cheered and hooted enthusiastically.

Adam waited until the dust cleared before going on. "You mean it's as though he was taking a different drug or not enough?" If Trent was keeping his dose of Ritalin and substituting something else to make it look like he was actually taking his medication, then he could stockpile the real drug and sell it to Marcus. It would also mean his self-control would be erratic, because he wouldn't be getting the chemical support when he needed it. It could explain the way he'd acted in English class, and what Zoë referred to as "episodes." Adam was excited now. He may have figured it out.

But Zoë was shaking her head adamantly. "No, I know he's taking his Ritalin, for sure."

Adam wondered how she could be so certain. "How do you know *for sure*? You said yourself he acts out as though he weren't getting his Ritalin."

"Promise you won't tell?" She leaned closer and Adam caught a trace of her perfume. The light flowery scent smelled great.

"What is it?" he asked, his voice dropping to a theatrical whisper.

Zoë's eyes darted around to make sure no one was listening. "When he's on his own, no medication…" She searched for the right words. "He … well, he *scratches* himself."

Adam was confused. "Scratches himself?"

"Yeah, you know…" She glanced down at Adam's crotch and he instantly flushed bright crimson. "Boy stuff…" She gave him an embarrassed smile. "He doesn't realize he's doing it at all. We can be standing in line at the opera and there'll be my big brother, rubbing his private parts. Thankfully, he doesn't do it on Ritalin, and he hasn't done it once lately, so I know he's well medicated." She giggled guiltily. "Please don't tell him. He can't help it. I'm sure it's some kind of unconscious compulsive behaviour and he would be mortified if he found out he's been looking like a pervert all these years."

Adam raised his eyebrows at this. "No worries. I'm not going to mention a word." He thought back over the last few times he and Trent had hung out. He hadn't seen him do anything like what Zoë was describing. That meant he was on his required dose of Ritalin, so how could he be taking his medication and selling large quantities at the same time?

"Can I ask you a question now?" Zoë wiggled around until she was facing him. "Do you really want to get back into all this again, or are you doing it because Trent wants you to? Is it because you were driving the night of the accident and you feel you owe him?"

The question caught Adam off guard. He was stunned that she could see through him so easily. He thought he'd sidetracked her earlier, but apparently Zoë Kendall wasn't one to be casually diverted.

She went on relentlessly. "I've seen the way you avoid getting into a car with him. In fact, the only time I've seen you two together in one was when you drove to the bottom of the driveway, then you threw up."

He flinched at the thought that she'd seen him puking his guts out. He felt like she could see into his mind. Adam was instantly defensive. "That's a wack question. I love rallying and this has nothing to do with owing your brother."

"Adam, if you feel guilty about the accident, you should talk to Trent. He knows it wasn't your fault. Don't forget, if it wasn't for the crash, he would never have been diagnosed with ADHD and been put on Ritalin. My best advice, friend to friend — stop feeling guilty and talk to Trent."

The image of Trent, his face cruelly scarred, limping up the school steps, exploded into Adam's mind. Sure, the accident had allowed him to be diagnosed with ADHD, but if he hadn't been diagnosed and put on drugs, he wouldn't have the lousy Ritalin to sell to Marcus now.

Everything was Adam's fault, didn't Zoë see that? Frustrated, angry, and defensive, he tried to turn the tables on her. "If we really want to talk about ulterior motives, what about you, Zoë? Why are you into rallying? Is it because you're tired of being the totally invisible Kendall kid and you want your dad to notice you?" Her eyes flew wide in shock as though he'd slapped her.

He instantly wished he could take the words back. He was being a jerk because she'd hit too close to the bone. His anger evaporated as quickly as it had come. "Oh man, I'm sorry, Zoë. That was totally out of line." He reached out and touched her arm. "I warned you that I suck. Can you forget I said that?"

She turned her deep green eyes to him and he thought he saw her expression soften a little, but knew the damage was done. He didn't know what else to say to make things better, so he tore his gaze away from her, avoiding the painful look in her eyes.

Taking a deep breath, Zoë stood up and dusted off her jeans. "I'm going to watch for Dad at the start of the next transit stage. Maybe he needs something." She walked away without a backward glance.

Adam knew he'd seriously screwed up. Zoë wasn't the problem here; he was. But all that would have to wait until later. The really huge issue now was Trent, his best friend and her only brother, being a drug dealer. He knew he had no choice left but to confront Trent. None of this was making sense to him, and the only person who knew all the answers was waiting back at the Evo.

Chapter 8

Adam didn't get a chance to talk to Trent that afternoon, as there were too many people around. When Mr. Kendall asked the drivers to come to his cabin for a barbecue that evening, Adam feared he wouldn't be able to get Trent alone at all. But it was Trent who said, "I don't want to hang around with these old fogies." He jerked his thumb in the direction of his father. "How would you like to go to a great place I know tonight? The music is wild and the wall-to-wall women are wilder."

They'd finished loading the Evo to be towed back to the cabin. Adam hoped that when Jorge diagnosed the broken wire on the injector, he'd chalk it up to simple mechanical failure and not look any further.

He could see Trent was wound up and itching to do something more exciting with his evening than sit around barbecuing burgers. Adam decided it would be cool to try something different. Also, going out would give him a chance to question Trent about Marcus and the drugs.

"Sounds like fun. I'll go home and clean up. If you give me the address, I can meet you there." He was glad he had his bike. He wasn't about to climb into a car with his friend now, not after everything he'd done to avoid it.

"The place is a converted warehouse in an industrial area, so there won't be any neon signs, but don't let appearances fool you. The place rocks!" Grinning, Trent gave him the address. "See you at nine."

Adam was sure he'd have a chance to talk to Trent at the club. His friend hadn't said anything about bringing a date, so that meant the two of them would be alone, at least until they scoped out a couple of likely ladies.

* * *

The technicolour light of the soft spring evening was fading as Adam rolled up to the club on his CBR. Trent had been right. No one would have taken this uninviting concrete and steel monolith as a hot spot.

Not the kind of place you'd want to be stranded at, Adam decided, pulling off his helmet. He was glad he had his own wheels in case Trent flew off the handle and deserted him. Accusing anyone of drug trafficking was dicey business, but when you were dealing with a chemically altered personality, who knew what might happen.

When Adam entered the darkened club, a solid wall of noise hit him like a tank. Everywhere, kids were laughing, talking, and moving to the sound. He could feel the rhythmic beat of the techno music vibrating through the soles of his sneakers and ratcheting into his bones. This was no ordinary night spot — if it weren't for the bouncers at the door and the servers wandering around with trays, this could have passed for a pretty decent rave.

Adam's assailed senses took a moment to process everything. A frenetically flashing strobe gave the place a surreal feel and made the gyrating dancers appear to blink on and off, as though a faulty film reel had gone berserk. The sickly sweet smell of marijuana drifted to him on the smoky haze.

Bumping his way through the crowd, Adam decided that the place must be on the shaky side of legal, if it was legal at all. When he finally made it past the frenzied dancers, he found Trent sitting at the bar.

"Hey, Adam! I'd just about given up on you. Since I'm legal, I'll order an extra beer for you." Trent signalled the bartender, who shook his head.

"But it's for me!" Trent protested innocently, but the bartender wasn't falling for that one. He pointed to a notice stating that picture ID was required as proof of age.

Adam looked at the empty glass on the counter. "Should you be having alcohol if you're taking Ritalin?" he asked. "I mean, is it safe?"

"Are you kidding? Relax, I know what I'm doing." Trent laughed at the concerned expression on Adam's face. "No worries, honest."

Despite Trent's assurances, Adam ordered colas for both of them. He had his own rules when it came to drinking. Even if he wasn't underage, he absolutely would never drink and drive, and that went double when he was on two wheels.

"Is there anywhere we can talk?" he asked Trent as soon as they had their drinks. He had to yell to be heard above the noise.

Trent grabbed his glass. "Follow me."

He led Adam to a series of small rooms at the back of the club. They were behind glass patio doors that muffled the noise enough that Adam didn't have to yell. He noticed that the purple and green vinyl seats had seen better days and one had a swatch of duct tape holding a split seam together.

"Take a load off." Trent slid into one side of the small booth. "Now, what's up? You want to discuss which rally we're entering next? I've got that all figured out. The Rocky Mountain Rally is being held at the end of May. I figure if we run a few more practice sessions, we can smooth out the rough spots and be a decently competitive team by then." He spoke rapidly and his eyes were glassy.

Adam wondered how much alcohol Trent had

already had, and if he was driving home.

"Wait a minute, Trent. We can discuss that later. Right now, I have something important to talk to you about." He wasn't sure how to begin, then decided the direct approach was the best. "I saw you with Marcus this morning."

Trent's forehead furrowed. "Yeah, so? I told you it was nothing."

Adam went on, "No, I mean I saw you giving the Ritalin to Marcus and I know it was Ritalin because I retrieved the bag and saw for myself. Trent, what's going on?" Adam waited for Trent to deny it, but instead his friend just took a long drink of his pop.

"You spying on me, old buddy?" His voice had taken on a taut edge that Adam didn't like.

"No, I happened to see you with Marcus, and you were arguing, so I watched to make sure everything was under control. That's when I saw you give Marcus the paper bag. I know how you feel about that creep and things didn't add up, so I thought I'd have a look for myself."

Trent slammed his glass down on the table. "My business is no concern of yours! Marcus and I go way back. He asked me to slip him some Ritalin to give him a little boost. He's been lagging behind in track and field, and said a hit of Ritalin might let him catch up on his training."

Adam thought this sounded bogus. "If he was using it himself, the amount I saw in that bag would do him for about ten years." He leaned

91

toward his friend. "I don't want you to end up in jail, Trent. I'm here for you and I want to help. Now, what's really going on?"

Adam saw the uncertainty in Trent's eyes, and then his friend's anger dissolved. He took a deep breath and blew it out noisily. Suddenly, he seemed immensely tired. "Okay, okay, I'll tell you what's going on. This is all my old man's fault."

Adam's eyebrows shot up in surprise. This wasn't what he'd expected to hear.

Trent went on, "When this whole Ritalin thing started, I told dear old dad I didn't want to do it. The idea of taking a drug for the rest of my life was bad enough, but a drug that flattens you out, turns you into a zombie, is something else." He took another sip of his drink. "When word got out I was on Ritalin, Marcus asked me to sell him a few. I figured if the old man was going to force me to take this crap, I might as well make a little money on it." Trent's shoulders slumped defeatedly. "The problem was, Marcus wasn't happy with just once. He wanted me to supply him indefinitely, for nothing."

He paused and Adam waited for him to go on, not wanting to break his friend's long-awaited talkative streak.

"He said if I didn't go along with his demands, he'd go to his cop father and say I was dealing. He said he'd claim that I tried to sell to him, but he turned me down, of course. Then he started asking for more of the stuff. I had to make it seem like my

ADHD was getting worse so my doctor would prescribe higher dosages and numbers of pills." His voice was bitter. "The doc was more than happy to up the amount I was on. I took the little I needed and banked the rest." Trent's pale sea-foam eyes glimmered with hidden pain. "The problem is that Marcus Dreger is never satisfied. He's been demanding more and more."

"Why don't you call his bluff? He has no proof." Adam gave Trent a meaningful look. "Does he?"

Trent slumped. "The first time I sold to Marcus, Gary Towes was with him. It's their word against mine. But how will it look? Marcus is a school sports hero and Gary is a stranger with no reason to lie. I have a crummy track record and have never been known as a good guy. There's no way Marcus's dad will let his kid go down."

He continued dispiritedly, "I told you my old man is going into politics. How would it look if his son were convicted of selling drugs? His political career would be dead in the water before it even got started."

Adam thought about everything that Trent had told him. Marcus was a local hero with a dad who was respected in the police department, and the fact that Marcus had a witness to Trent's selling was a tough one to beat. It didn't look good for Trent, but Adam wasn't going to write his friend off so easily. "I'm not giving up or giving in. Let me work on this, but in the meantime, do yourself a favour — *stop supplying Marcus*. Stall him. Give him some excuse until we can figure out how to get you out of this mess."

Trent sighed with relief. "Okay, I'll stop. We can work together, but you can't say a word about this to anyone. Promise?"

Adam hesitated, thinking he'd like to talk to his dad, then reluctantly agreed. "I promise."

Their glasses were empty and Adam couldn't see a server anywhere. "Come on, we'll get another cola and check out the women. You said they were wild, and wall to wall. I want to see for myself." He grinned at Trent.

Heading to the bar, they were dodging their way though the packed bodies when Trent stopped short, staring. Adam followed his gaze and groaned.

Zoë was on the dance floor, wearing a very short mini-skirt and a provocatively tight shirt with suggestive cutouts. And she wasn't alone. Marcus Dreger was with her. They were laughing and seemed to be having a great time.

Adam could see Trent tense up. His friend's face grew red, the jagged scar practically glowing with heat as he began cursing. Before Adam could stop him, Trent angrily shoved his way through the crowd toward Zoë and Marcus.

He reached Marcus and grabbed him by the arm, spinning him around. "What the hell do you think you're doing with my sister, Dreger?"

Marcus's eyes were half-shut and his speech

was a little slurred when he spoke. "Well if it isn't my best friend Trent. Hey, your little sister is hot…"

Adam stepped in. "That's enough, Marcus! Are you crazy? Zoë's not part of your crowd. And what are you doing with a kid like her in the first place?" He heard the anger in his own voice.

Adam noticed Zoë's eyes were glazed. "Zoë, are you all right?" he asked. "Have you been drinking?"

Zoë's head lolled sideways as she answered, "All I've had is this fun drink that Marcus got me." She held up a small neon-coloured baby bottle with liquid in it.

Trent took one look at his sister and turned on Marcus. "Did you slip her something, you son-of-a—"

"Hey, it's not my fault if little sister wants a real man to take care of her." Marcus leered at Zoë. "And I plan on taking good care of her."

"Like hell!" Trent turned back to Zoë and took her arm. "Come on. We're getting out of here."

Zoë shook her head jerkily, wrenching her arm out of Trent's grasp. "Let go! I don't want to leave. Marcus is my date tonight and I don't need you pulling the big brother routine now." She tried to stand straight, but swayed unsteadily on her high heels. "For months, all I've heard about was poor Trent, tragically scarred in the accident; poor Trent, who will never walk normally again; and poor Trent with ADHD! All Mom and Dad talk about is you, and you love it! You do everything you can to make sure you stay the centre of the universe. Well, tonight *I'm* the centre of the universe." She smiled lopsidedly at her date. "At least the centre of Marcus's universe, right, Marcus?"

Momentarily speechless, Trent stared at her. "Where is this crap coming from, Zoë? You never said a word."

Zoë ineffectually tried to push her hair behind her ear. "That's the point. I *never* say a word. Do you think I like sitting on the sidelines and watching all those rally practices, or listening to you and Dad drone on about cars and gears like I'm too dumb to understand? I do it so I'll at least be noticed as existing in the Kendall house." She waved her hand absently. "Now, get lost. I'm staying."

Trent moved between his sister and Marcus, pleading with her. "Zoë, I don't trust this jerk. Be reasonable and come home with me."

"She said she wants to stay!" Marcus's voice was loud, and several people nearby had started watching.

"Hey, back off, creep!" one guy yelled at Trent.

"Somebody call the bouncers!" another added.

"Take a hike, big brother," Marcus jeered.

Trent whirled on Marcus and grabbed his shirt. "She's my sister and she's leaving with me."

Marcus pushed Trent's hand away. "You belong in a padded cell!"

Before Adam could stop him, Trent took a swing

at Marcus, hitting him squarely in the mouth. Blood gushed from Marcus's split lip.

Adam held Trent's arm, trying to pull him away. "Cool it, Trent!" But his friend was out of control and lunged for Marcus again. Adam wrestled with him, trying to keep himself between Trent and his target.

Marcus tentatively touched his swollen lip, then looked at the blood on his fingers. "You freak. You'll pay for this."

Two burly bouncers appeared out of the crowd and grabbed both Marcus and Trent by the arms. "What's going on here, you two?" the bigger of the two asked in a guttural voice.

"This punk's feeding my sister booze and she's underage!" Trent yelled.

The bouncer eyed Zoë, who was now showing obvious signs that she'd been drinking but who certainly didn't look underage. "Do you have any identification, Miss?" he asked.

Zoë squirmed with embarrassment. "Ah, it's in my other purse." She mumbled, her voice slurred.

The smaller bouncer took a closer look at Marcus. Recognizing him, he immediately dropped his hold. "Is she with you, Marc?"

"Hey, I had no idea she was underage." Marcus held his hands up.

"I'm afraid if she has no ID, I'm going to have to ask her to leave." The bouncer shuffled his feet uncomfortably.

Marcus cursed under his breath. "This is not

how I planned my Saturday night to end." He grabbed Zoë by the hand and began leading her off the dance floor.

"I'm right behind you, Dreger, so you can take her straight home." Trent trailed his sister and her date out of the club.

Adam followed. He wondered if part of this was his fault. Maybe what he had said to Zoë had triggered her hidden resentment of her brother. She had to know that going out with Marcus would really tick off Trent. One thing was for sure. This was turning into a complicated situation.

Chapter 9

The next week at school, Trent had another spectacular run-in with a teacher. Everyone was talking about how Trent had told off Ms. Hedley and how she'd hauled him to the counsellor's office for a little private session. Adam wondered if Trent needed extra drugs and was making himself appear worse than he was to get them. After their talk, he hoped Trent wasn't continuing to supply Marcus.

Adam talked to his dad about "a friend," mentioning no names, who had a problem. Without divulging too many details, he asked his father's advice.

"I figure this *friend* should face up to and solve his own problems without involving you. Your mother and I don't want to see you heading down that path again."

Adam knew his dad had figured out whom they were talking about.

Mr. Harlow put a comforting hand on Adam's shoulder. "But I'm darn proud of you for sticking by your friend, son. It's the right thing to do. Just make sure he makes the wise choice this time." This made Adam feel better but didn't fix his problem.

Trent invited Adam out to the cabin, which would have been a great time to talk, but Adam couldn't face the prospect of taking out the Evo and declined.

Walking toward his locker at school, Adam saw Zoë coming down the hallway. Here was a problem he could do something about. He blocked her path.

"Zoë, I'm sorry about what happened Saturday night. I didn't know Trent was going to flip out like that."

She glared at him frostily, shifting her armload of books. "Yeah, the timing sucked. I'd really been looking forward to that date. Marcus and I've been out several times and we always have a blast." She let this hang in the air between them.

Adam wanted to tell Zoë that Marcus was a no-good creep, who was, at the least, using Ritalin to enhance his track performance, and, at the worst, a drug-dealing scum blackmailer. But he'd promised Trent he wouldn't say anything, so instead he decided to try and smooth things over between Zoë and her brother.

"Trent is only looking out for you. He loves you and he's doing what he thinks is best. When we saw you on Saturday, you seemed zoned out, like you were stoned or drunk. Trent was worried, that's all, and he's right to be. Marcus Dreger is bad news." He wanted her to believe him, to put things right between her and Trent.

"I think my brother is jealous of Marcus." Zoë's voice had a hard edge. "Marcus is popular, good-looking and, on top of being the school track star, he's a fabulous driver. Did you know he and Gary travel all over the U.S. and Canada rallying? He says if he keeps finishing in the money, his dad is going to help him go professional next season."

She relaxed a little, her voice softening. "Look, for what it's worth, you're right. I wasn't myself on Saturday. I don't even remember most of what I said to Trent." She took a deep breath, her expression troubled. "Maybe Marcus did add something to my drink. But I'm a big girl; I'll deal with him myself. I don't need Trent riding in and pulling the big-brother routine."

Her face was all cool confidence, but Adam heard the tremor in her voice and wondered if she was worried about what Marcus had done. He smiled reassuringly at her. "That's what big brothers do."

She shook her head. "Too little, too late." She hesitated as though deciding something. "Look, you remember that first day you came over to visit?"

Adam nodded.

"And Trent thought you'd called him but really

101

I'd set it up? The reason I wanted you to come over was because I was hoping if you and my big brother got together again, he'd be so busy with guy things that maybe it would be more normal around our place. Right now, every time Trent sneezes, it's a major family crisis." She sighed. "I guess on Saturday night, I'd had enough for one day and that's when I told Trent off. Did you know Marcus's dad phoned our house the next morning?"

"About the fight?" Adam asked.

"He warned my father that if his out-of-control son went wild and attacked Marcus again, he'd have him arrested. He yelled so loudly I could hear him from across the room. Trent came off looking like a major goon."

"Man, that's just what Trent needs right now." Adam knew this was unfair to his friend. He would have done the same thing if it had been his little sister. In fact he definitely had no problem stepping up for Zoë at any time.

Zoë looked at him and Adam thought he saw something odd in her expression, almost hopeful. "See you on the weekend?" she asked. "The Forest Service has shut down a big section of the Powderface Trail to put in a power line and, since it's adjacent to our property, Dad's got permission to test the STi on it. Now Trent's fired up to climb behind the wheel of the Evo and see if he still has those razor-sharp skills he loves to go on and on about. I'm sure he's expecting you to co-drive." She tipped her head sideways, looking incredibly vulnerable and appealing. "I'll let you in on a little secret. I didn't mean all that stuff I said on Saturday. I kind of like rallying; in fact, I like it a lot. It would be cool if you were there." She smiled shyly and hugged her books. "Because the truth is, I like you a lot too."

Adam didn't know what to say. He now wanted to be at the Kendalls' on the weekend in a big way. His stomach twinged ominously at the thought. He hadn't a clue what excuse he'd come up with to get out of riding with Trent, but this was one invitation he couldn't turn down. "I wouldn't miss it." He smiled back at Zoë and they stood grinning at each other for what seemed like a long time.

"See ya," Zoë said softly and walked away.

Adam watched her go, noticing the graceful way she moved. He knew he would soon have no choice but to tell Trent he couldn't rally with him. Putting the Evo out of commission at the race had made him feel like a real lowlife. He'd cheated Trent out of a great ride. If he made up some excuse as to why he couldn't rally anymore, Trent could find someone else to co-drive. That way, at least one of them would get to live out his dream.

* * *

That Friday, Adam met Trent moving quickly down the school hallway at lunch. He looked awkward and off balance as he swung his leg out to hurry along. "Where've you been, Adam? I've got big news." His face was flushed and Adam wondered if it was time for another pill.

"If this is about coming out to the cabin tomorrow, don't worry, I'll be there." Adam had thought of an ingenious way of solving two problems with one ride.

Trent hesitated as though shifting gears. "Right, of course you're coming out tomorrow. This has nothing to do with tomorrow. This has to do with all my tomorrows!" He was practically bouncing off the walls. "You remember that chemistry project I was working on for Mr. P.? It was near and dear to my heart, because it had to do with making an additive to increase the viscosity of engine oil used in racing so it won't break down under the high temperatures and pressures." He inhaled loudly, filling his lungs before charging on. "Long story short, the old dog sent it and a couple of my other experiments off to some special committee and they've been corresponding and checking my grades. What it all means is the scholarship I applied for months ago but didn't think I had a hope in hell of winning, well, Adam old buddy…" He pummelled Adam playfully in the stomach. "You're never going to believe this, but I've been awarded a full scholarship to McGill University's accelerated chemistry program! This is every science geek's dream! Man, I am beyond pumped! Zoë's in the library. I know she's still ticked with me, but I want her to hear this. Can you find her and drag her to our locker? I'm going to get my cell phone and call my mom."

"This is huge!" Adam had never seen Trent so happy. "You go phone your mom *and dad*, and I'll get Zoë."

Adam hurried toward the library. Trent had talked about the chemistry program offered at McGill, but with his disciplinary record, he hadn't thought he had a chance of getting in. Adam smiled. Well, he was in now! Wow, his friend was going to be famous, and no one deserved it more.

Adam walked into the library and started looking for Zoë in the stacks. He didn't have to look far. She barrelled around the corner of a shelf and practically ran him over. "Whoa! Just the person I'm looking for!" Then he noticed her angry expression. "What's up? You look ready to kill someone." He saw that her eyes were red and she'd been crying. "Zoë, what's wrong? Are you okay?"

Surprised to see him, she swiped at her wet cheeks, ignoring his questions. "Adam, what are you doing here?"

He noticed her lip quivering. She wouldn't look at him. "Trent wants to tell you something important. He asked me to get you."

"I've about had it with pushy guys, Adam. No thanks." She sniffed loudly as she tried to move past him.

Adam touched her on the arm. "It's important Zoë, honest."

She took a deep breath. "Oh, all right. Where is the little prince?"

"He's waiting at our locker." Before he could

say anything else, Zoë hurried past him and out of the library. Adam turned to follow.

Out of the corner of his eye, he caught a glimpse of Marcus Dreger leaving through the other door.

Adam caught up with Zoë. "He's calling your parents."

"What is it? Is he in trouble again?" She glanced at Adam apprehensively.

"No, just the opposite." Adam took her hand. "No time for more questions. Come on!"

Together they ran to the locker where Trent was just shutting off his cell phone.

His eyes twinkled mischievously. "Hi there, little sister." He paused while she gave him an exasperated look, then he grinned. "Guess whose big brother is going to McGill's accelerated chemistry program on a full scholarship?" he asked before Zoë could say anything.

She stopped, her eyes wide, then she turned to Adam for confirmation.

"It's true. Scout's honour," Adam answered with mock seriousness.

Zoë's face broke into a wide grin. She had known of Trent's dream of going to the prestigious school. "No way! This is so cool! I'll be able to go shopping in Montreal when I come to visit!" she teased. She hugged her brother, their former fight forgotten. "This is so great, Trent. I know how badly you wanted this. Congratulations."

Adam hoped this award would help Trent and

his dad make up. What father wouldn't be proud of his son winning a full scholarship?

* * *

The ride out to the cabin was sweet. The weather was hot and sultry, and the road empty of traffic, allowing Adam to open up his CBR. He felt good about this visit and could hardly wait to put his plan into play. Roaring up on his motorbike, Adam parked beside the Evo. Jorge was standing, arms crossed, staring at the rally car.

"Something the matter?" Adam asked, hoping the car still wasn't driveable.

"No, nothing." Jorge tipped his head at the car. "In fact, if the Evo was running this well when Steven was driving it, he might not have dropped the bundle on the STi."

Adam's hopes of an easy out evaporated. "Did you ever figure out what happened to it at the rally?" He hoped Jorge didn't suspect anything.

Jorge shook his head. "Craziest thing. One of the leads on the injectors was broken, not worn, just snapped in two as cleanly as though it had been cut. Strange." He smiled wryly at Adam. "Maybe a joke of the racing gods, eh?"

Relieved his sabotage had gone undetected, Adam retreated to the cabin.

The family was gathered in the study and Zoë called him in, handing him a glass of iced tea. She moved beside him and Adam was acutely aware of her nearness. He felt a buzzing sensation, as though he was standing too close to a strong electric current. The subtle scent of her perfume made him want to close his eyes and breathe deeply. Not wanting his thoughts to continue in the direction they were going, he tried to distract himself by checking out the study.

Adam had always liked this room. It was user-friendly. Crowded with family pictures in ornate frames, overstuffed furniture, and richly woven carpets, it was warm and inviting. One wall was covered in tall bookshelves that reached to the top of the four-metre ceiling. A rolling ladder allowed access to the highest books. The opposite side of the study had huge windows running the full height of the wall, with French doors leading out to a flagstone patio. The view was spectacular. The manicured lawn, edged by towering pines, ran down to a pond with a small waterfall. It was a peaceful scene and made Adam feel good. He refocused on Mr. Kendall, who was speaking.

"...And if you apply yourself, this could open up incredible opportunities for you," Trent's father went on. "Of course, once you've graduated, the competition will be stiff for the good jobs and you never know how things will work out. To finish well, you'll have to work harder than you've ever worked in your life. From past experience, we know this could be a formidable challenge..." He pursed his lips and let this hang.

"Nonsense, Steven!" Mrs. Kendall interrupted

as she went to stand beside her son. "Trent is going to do a wonderful job. Of course he knows it will be challenging, but he has a gift when it comes to his chemistry and now he has a goal. I'm sure he's going to be a brilliant success!"

Trent glowed under his mom's praise. This was more than the scholarship; it was proving he was capable of doing something totally great. Whatever Trent had done wrong in the past, this had to go a long way in redeeming himself in his parents' eyes.

"Trent, if you want this, you have the power to make it happen, but it's going to be up to you *and only you*." Mr. Kendall poured himself a drink from the liquor cart. His tone softened as he raised his glass. "Here's to gifts and goals, son."

"To gifts and goals!" everyone agreed, raising their glasses in a toast to Trent.

After discussing every detail of the scholarship, conversation naturally returned to rallying and cars.

"I'm sure you boys will have a great ride today. Jorge's been fussing over that car all week." Mr. Kendall reached into his pocket and withdrew a set of keys for the Evo, handing them to Trent. "Zoë's been studying the pace notes on the Powderface. I'll get them from the desk in the living room." He left, returned a moment later with a sheaf of papers, and handed them to Adam. "You should go over these in detail before you take that car out."

Adam held the notes in a death grip, swallowing as the panic filled his throat like sulphuric acid. Smiling weakly, he hoped his plan would work. "This weekend is a Kendall celebration and, in keeping with that spirit, I think Zoë should be Trent's co-driver today. Besides, she's been over the notes and knows them cold. If Trent wants to really put that car through its paces, he'll need someone fast on directions. I can go next time." He handed the papers to Zoë and her face lit up.

At first Adam thought Trent was going to say no again. Instead, he turned and started for the door. "Let's go, Zoë! Man, I hope you don't get airsick!"

Adam enjoyed watching the Evo speed down the long curving driveway. Brother and sister were back on good terms, and he had avoided getting into a rally car with Trent one more time.

Chapter 10

"I need to talk to you. Can you meet me for lunch?" Zoë's voice on the phone sounded upset.

"What's the matter?" Adam asked, concerned. He could hear her hesitation and wondered if she was upset. "I've been meaning to come over, but I've been struggling to catch up on my school-work. I sort of fell behind when I was in Saudi." When Zoë didn't say anything, he blundered on, trying to explain. "And last weekend, I had to help Mom and Dad with the yardwork." He felt guilty, he hadn't seen much of Zoë or Trent except for brief connections at school. He'd tried to get together with Trent to figure out a plan, but his friend kept coming up with excuses, saying he was busy or would call him back. Adam knew Trent was dodging him and worried it was because of Marcus and the drugs.

"Jeez, Adam, chill! Nothing's the matter. I just thought you might be free and since it's Saturday…"

Her voice trailed off and Adam wondered if there was something else on Zoë's mind.

He glanced at his watch. "Your big brother ditched me again today, so I'm heading to the Chinook Mall alone to see the Toys for Boys exhibit. They've got a lot of fast cars on display that I'm planning on checking out. I'd love company, and it would give us a chance to grab a hot dog and talk."

"Oh, yuck!" Zoë sounded disgusted.

Adam wondered what he'd said, then remembered she was a staunch vegetarian. He could practically see her nose wrinkling in disgust at the thought of a hot dog.

"Sorry, I forgot — 'nothing that had parents.' We could find you a veggie delight or stale bread and water somewhere," he laughed. "See you in an hour."

The large mall was jammed with parents, kids, and — best of all — cars. The exhibits covered everything from Formula Atlantics, built for speed with their sleek aerodynamic open-wheel design, to hybrid electric cars that would make the trip to work fuel-efficient, quiet, and, Adam suspected, very boring.

"So what's up?" Adam glanced at Zoë as he checked the specs on a nitrous-fuelled funny car, which purported to have over five thousand horsepower.

They moved to the front of a lime-green sprint car. Zoë studiously avoided his gaze as she inspected its tall, exaggerated wing. Her voice sounded strained to Adam as she avoided his question. "It's too bad Trent isn't here. This is absolutely his kind of stuff."

They moved on to the next display, featuring a mini-dragster. Neither of them spoke as they studied the car. Finally, she turned to him, letting her hand rest against his as though she could draw strength from the touch. "Adam, I think Trent is having some kind of serious meltdown."

Adam could sense her tension. "What do you mean, 'meltdown'?" He was instantly apprehensive. At school, Trent had seemed a little wilder than usual, but Adam had chalked that up to his excitement over the scholarship. Had things somehow escalated between Marcus and Trent? Maybe one of their deals had gone wrong.

"He's worse than I've ever seen him." She folded her arms as though holding herself for comfort. "It's like he's out of control. One minute he's bouncing off the ceiling, then he's so depressed he won't come out of his room." She turned to face him. "The school called. Trent's behaviour has been so erratic, the principal is worried his scholarship may be in jeopardy. Adam, if they take that away from Trent, it will kill him." The quicksilver tears that had been glistening at the corners of her eyes now slipped down her cheeks. "I don't know how to help him."

Things were way worse than Adam had suspected. He put an arm around her. "Hey, hold on.

Maybe we can figure out what's happening. I'm sure if we put our minds to it, we can help Trent. I'll talk to him, see what I can find out." Drug dealing would make any sane teenager melt down. He'd heard the usual news flashes at school about Trent wigging out on a teacher and doing crazy things. He had noticed that Trent seemed more stressed than usual when they'd gone to class together or met at their locker, but it was sometimes hard to tell what was going on with his friend.

Adam took Zoë's hand and they wandered over to a line of fast motorcycles. The road racing, moto-cross, and drag racing bikes were lined up as if you could pick your favourite and put it in your shopping cart.

He wanted to tell her about the drugs and how Marcus was putting pressure on her brother, but he'd promised not to say anything. Besides, he knew that something that big should come from Trent. He would totally impress her if he could come up with an instant solution to the whole mess, but that wasn't on the table right now.

Zoë still seemed very upset. "Are you telling me everything?" he asked.

Zoë took a tissue out of her leather shoulder bag and wiped her nose. "Nothing you can help me with."

He took her over to a bench beside a shiny 400 hp Corvette Z06. "Why don't you try me? I'm a pretty resourceful guy."

Zoë took a long shuddering breath. "It's Marcus." Adam tensed. "He won't leave me alone."

He looked at her sharply. "What do you mean, 'he won't leave you alone'? I thought he was your dream date."

She gave him a quick scowl. "I thought he was too. But, well…" She took another deep breath. "We were out together, and Marcus met up with two junior high kids. They started talking about a score and, before I realized what was happening, Marcus pulls out a bottle of pills. He sells the stuff to the two guys and pockets the money. He was so cool, like this is something he does all the time. It freaked me out."

She sniffed loudly. "I have a real thing about illegal drugs, Adam. I won't have anything to do with someone who uses or sells. I told Marcus we were through, but he laughed and said he was the one calling the shots and would let me know when we were done."

She turned to Adam, her tear-stained face red and blotchy. "Adam, he's been stalking me. He calls at all hours and follows me, and he's left sick suggestive notes on my locker. Yesterday, he sat behind me in a movie theatre and nearly gave me a heart attack. The guy's a nutcase. I told him to leave me alone or I'd go to the authorities and tell them I saw him selling drugs. He laughed. He said it would look like I made it up for revenge because of the fight he and Trent had over me at the club. He said he has a dozen witnesses to the fight, including the bouncers."

Adam was speechless.

Zoë grabbed his arm, squeezing tightly. "You have to promise not to say anything to Trent. The way he's acting lately, he'll go crazy and do something to Marcus."

Adam knew the whole situation was now different because of what Marcus was doing to Zoë. "Zoë, I can't promise anything like that. This is serious. You have to tell your parents."

She shook her head adamantly. "No! I don't want my folks dragged into my problems. My dad doesn't need the bad headlines. I would feel terrible if I caused him any public embarrassment, especially over a creepy jerk like Marcus."

Adam covered her hand protectively with his and gave it a squeeze. "Listen to me. This is nothing to fool around with. Talk to Trent; he'll tell you about Marcus. Both of you should put your cards on the table."

She stared at him, first surprised, then suspicious. "What cards does Trent have that I don't know about?"

Adam wanted to tell her about Marcus and the drugs, but was bound by his promise. "I … I think you two should talk, that's all," he stammered.

Zoë sighed resignedly. "No, I can handle my own problems. Right now, I'm more concerned with Trent. You're the best friend he has. Can you talk to him, find out what's wrong?"

Adam wished he hadn't promised both Zoë and

Trent not to talk to anyone about what was going on. He could use his dad's advice. For weeks now, Adam had been reassuring his father that on Ritalin Trent was as normal as any other teenager. His dad had laughed and said that perhaps that was the problem. Unfortunately, for all of them, the problems were now past the realm of normal teenage trouble.

As Adam walked Zoë to her car, it was as though he was standing on spring ice and a Chinook had just blown in. Everything was going to crack wide open at any minute with disastrous results.

He had no choice now. He had to convince Trent to go to the police and tell them everything. Marcus was dangerous.

Chapter 11

Adam called Trent and asked to meet him at a local park. Sitting on a bench beside the river, they watched several Canada geese picking at the grass. The large birds waddled about comically, browsing on the lawn, trimming it to the evenness of the smooth, green felt on a pool table.

Trent seemed exhausted and he had dark smudges under his eyes. "Okay, what's up? What do you want to talk about?" His hand opened and closed reflexively in an agitated way.

Adam looked at Trent, surprised. "What do you think? You look like hell; your sister's worried sick about you; and the school's phoning your parents about your wild behaviour. You've been ditching me for two weeks. What's going on?"

Trent shook his head abstractedly. "No worries. I've been busy, that's all." Absently, he gave his groin a scratch.

Adam instantly flashed on what Zoë had told

him. "That's it, no more garbage about being busy! I want the truth." He looked Trent straight in the eye. "Is Marcus demanding so much Ritalin that you've had to give him your own pills? Are you under-medicating yourself so you can supply that wack job?"

"I'm handling things!" Trent exploded. "I just need a little more time to figure everything out."

"What do you have to figure out? Trent, you've got to go to the police about Marcus. The guy is poison." Adam was desperate. "Maybe if you talk to your dad, he can help."

"Help? This will be the final straw. You don't understand, Adam." Trent hung his head in his hands. It was as though the will to fight had simply bled out of him. "I took your advice. I went to Marcus and told him I couldn't do it any more. To make up the numbers he wanted, I've had to kick in my own dosage and it's making me come apart at the seams. Marcus laughed and said he had a better idea. He'll forget about the extra Ritalin, and in exchange all I have to do is build him methamphetamine instead. He heard about the chemistry scholarship and knows I can do it. Getting hold of the raw ingredients is easy. You can pick most of them up at the local hardware store."

"He wants you to build *ice*?" Adam was shocked. He stood up and began pacing; startling the geese who honked and flapped, indignant at having their foraging disturbed. "*Crank*? For God's sake Trent, this is too much. That junk is seriously dangerous stuff. We have to go to the cops."

"No cops!" Trent's voice cracked. "They'll never believe me."

Adam saw the silent pleading in his friend's eyes and sat back down next to him.

Trent took a deep breath, then exhaled loudly. "Do you remember when I said I once asked my old man to get me out of a tough jam?"

"Yes," Adam answered, wondering where this was leading.

"It wasn't kid's stuff. It happened before I knew you." He squirmed uncomfortably on the bench. "I was busted for possession of marijuana when I was fourteen. I didn't know what it was when a buddy asked me to hold a package, but the cops didn't believe me. Finally, it was proven I wasn't in on it, but because I had a high-priced defence lawyer for a father, I knew everyone would think I just got away with it. I begged my old man to pull some strings and get it hushed up. I was enough of a freak at school without adding a possession charge to my list of endearing qualities. Take that piece of history, combine it with Gary Towes backing Marcus about the first drug deal; add the fight at the club — and the end result is I'm finished.

"I'm eighteen now, an adult. It's a whole other ball game. Marcus's dad will make it look like *I'm* the lifer bad guy here and his kid is the poor victim. The tabloids will have a field day, and my old man's political career will be in the toilet. After everything I've done, this would finish our family, and it would all be because of me. The best I can hope for is to give Marcus the meth and tell him it's a one-shot deal, no repeat offers." He rubbed his eyes tiredly. "If all this comes out, there's no way McGill will take me. I stand to lose a lot more than Marcus does, and he knows it."

Adam couldn't believe what he was hearing. "You're kidding, right? You know Marcus will never let you out from under his hammer. He'll keep upping the ante. You've got to stop him here, now. You can't let Marcus win."

Trent ignored him, staring at the light reflecting off the water. Adam had one more card to play and he hoped it would be an ace. "There's something else you need to know." He knew Zoë would never forgive him, but he had to do something drastic to get Trent to stop Marcus. "Marcus is stalking Zoë."

Instantly, he had Trent's full attention. Trent's head snapped around. "What?"

"Zoë tried to dump Marcus after he sold drugs to a couple of young kids right in front of her. He won't let her go. He keeps following her around and freaking her out." Adam sat back on the bench letting this sink in. "We have to do something — if not for your sake, then for Zoë's."

"That rotten son-of-a-..." It was Trent's turn to clamber to his feet. He started hobbling up and down anxiously, his agitation building like a volcano getting ready to erupt. "He's gone too far this time. If he gets his hooks into my sister, I can just guess what he'll want from her." Adam had never seen Trent so angry. The cords in his neck were standing out like cables. "Okay, I'm in. What can we do to tear his world apart?"

Adam felt relieved. Trent's face radiated energy; he was a man on a mission. This was the wild and wired Trent that Adam remembered from before the Ritalin, but with a subtle difference — now he had a focus for all that energy. Adam knew that once his buddy set his sights on a target, good or bad, nothing could sway him.

Adam remembered that when Marcus's car had broken an axle at the rally, he had thought of racing as a force of nature, one of those things beyond your control. Before the accident, Trent was like that, behaving as though he had no choice in what he did. Perhaps it was because of his ADHD, but he never stopped himself, never backed down. He would blow petty things out of proportion, especially when it came to his tumultuous relationship with his father. Trent always looked for the worst in anything his dad said or did, and then he would respond by simply reacting badly without thought to the consequences.

Adam realized how much Trent had changed since then. The old Trent was still there, but now he had a rev-limiter that would help him harness his horsepower. He had joined the race, and it gave Adam new hope for his friend.

"That's more like it!" Adam jumped up and

stood beside Trent. "Once you focus all that heat of yours at a target, nothing can stop you." He thought for a moment. "Your folks' cabin is deserted this weekend, right?"

"Yes, as a matter of fact, it is. The Forestry Service is digging everything up and there's no electricity, no phones, no nothing. My folks can't be without a microwave or a modem, so they're staying in the city."

"Good. You'll tell Marcus that you have the ice and will be at the cabin on Saturday. He has to come out and pick it up." Adam knew it would take more than the two of them joining forces to convince Marcus the deal was off, and he'd come up with a plan he thought would work. Would *have to* work. "And when he does, we'll record the event with your dad's camcorder. We'll tell him his drug dealing days are over, and that if he doesn't stop harassing Zoë, we'll go to your father, the big-shot lawyer, and show him the video. The decision will be Marcus's. He can walk away clean or there'll be a bloodbath."

"And what if he calls my bluff?" Trent asked.

Adam turned to him, his face deadly serious. "That's the point. You won't be bluffing."

Chapter 12

Adam watched as Trent paced in front of the big stone fireplace in the sunken living room of the spacious cabin. He was back on his Ritalin, and Adam hoped it would help him think more clearly. Outside the large picture windows, the late afternoon sun was losing the battle to the ominously rumbling black clouds. In the failing light, Adam felt like he was in a scene out of a bad movie.

Nervously, Trent kept looking down the long twisting driveway for any sign of Marcus. "Maybe we should jump him when he gets here and beat the crap out of him. That would persuade him to get lost in a big hurry."

Adam looked at his friend nervously, trying to assess his condition. Had he been wrong about Trent being back on his meds and under control?

Then Trent's face split into a wide grin. "Psych! Don't worry. I'm in enough trouble without adding assault to the growing list."

Adam glanced at his watch. "Marcus should be here any minute. He won't try anything with the two of us staring him in the face. If he does, it will all be recorded for posterity." He moved to the mantle and rechecked the tiny audio-video camera, hidden among the pictures. "We have to make sure the jerk is in range of the camera before we start quizzing him."

The sound of an engine revving, then silence, announced Marcus's arrival. "Ready?" Adam asked, checking out the window, then switching on the tiny recorder. Marcus had parked his sleek silver BMW 330 beside Trent's car and was walking toward the cabin.

"I'd better be." Trent ran his hand through his hair nervously and limped to the door to let Marcus Dreger in.

Marcus stepped into the room and stopped, his eyes narrowing when he saw Adam. "Well, isn't this cosy." He dropped onto the couch glaring at Adam, then turned to Trent. "What's he doing here?"

Trent sounded casual. "You didn't think I'd be dumb enough to meet you here alone, did you? Besides, Adam's cool about everything."

Marcus seemed to evaluate this for a moment. "Okay, fine, your little buddy can stay. Since you interrupted my plans and made me drive to this God-forsaken place, I don't have time for social niceties. Get the stuff so I can leave. We'll discuss your next delivery later."

"Marcus, you have a great set-up here," said Adam, trying to look confident and at ease, arms folded across his chest. He was sitting in an easy chair by the fireplace, so Marcus had to turn toward the camera to answer him. Marcus was in the perfect position for everything to be caught by the camera. Now all they had to do was get him to be specific about the drug dealing. "I have to hand it to you, this is going to be one sweet deal." He could see Marcus start to relax under the praise. "You convince Trent to give you his Ritalin, so you can sell it or take it yourself to stay the track star, and then you have the brilliant idea to have him go that one step further and build you meth. It's not exactly like he can say no, because you and Gary can burn him to the ground with that first score you made. He did sell you the Ritalin.

"But what I can't figure out is how you sell the drugs without anyone getting suspicious?" Adam held his breath, hoping Marcus's ego would kick in. In his expensive black cashmere sweater and black chinos, the guy could have passed for a junior Mafioso.

"You know, Harlow, one day that curiosity of yours is going to put you in the ground, but because I'm such a nice guy, I think I'll ease your misery and explain how things work in the real world." Marcus leaned back and put his hands behind his head. "I do have the perfect set-up. Gary and I travel all over through our rallying, and at each stop, mixed in with the adoring fans, we

126

meet a few regular customers. No one suspects a thing. This year, we even expanded into the States and have had no trouble at the border, since we're legit rally drivers." He smiled smugly. "I make a lot of money selling this crap to losers, a lot of money."

"You know, Marcus, I have a strong feeling all that is about to come to an abrupt end." Adam smiled coolly back at Marcus, then tipped his head at Trent. "Did you want to add anything?"

Trent's jaw tightened as he took a step forward. "I think it's time you found out how things work in *our* world, Dreger. Like the fact that there is no meth, and there never will be. There also won't be any more Ritalin. In fact, as far as you and I are concerned, consider this an end to our arrangement."

Marcus went very still, and then his face grew dark. "You stupid punk. Do you think you're in a position to tell me what we're going to do?" His eyes were reptilian slits. "I call the shots around here, not you."

Adam moved over to stand beside Trent. "Not any more, Marcus. It's two against one now."

Marcus was on his feet in an instant, the intensity of his rage hitting them like a shock wave. "Aren't you forgetting what would happen if dear old dad found out you've been dealing drugs? I doubt if the good citizens of Alberta would vote for a guy with a convicted dope dealer for a son." His voice had a note of triumph as he went on. "A son with a bad track record for consorting with known pot heads." He laughed coldly. "Yeah, my dad told me all about your past. Even your old man couldn't keep something that hot under wraps, no matter how hard he tried to bury it."

"I was never charged and you know it!" Trent was furious.

Marcus went on relentlessly. "It's how it looks, Trent, my boy. People will think where there's smoke, there's fire. What else has your fancy lawyer dad hushed up? Not really a platform many politicians want to go to the polls with." His steely blue eyes glittered dangerously in the gloomy light.

Trent pulled himself up to his full height. "My dad didn't do anything wrong. I was the one who messed up and, since I'm here with you, I guess you could say I'm a slow learner." He took a limping step toward Marcus. "I am a screw-up, but I'm fixing that right now. And if you think I won't come clean about everything in order to put you behind bars, that's where you've made a big mistake. I have no problem with paying my dues. What would your father, the hotshot cop, think if his golden boy track hero ended up a criminal behind bars?"

Adam thought he saw Marcus hesitate and jumped in to hammer the point home. This was obviously Marcus's weak spot. "And with me backing up his story, I think there'll be enough doubt that the authorities will be looking long and hard at your past too. Maybe your dad will find out what his star athlete son does on the side." Marcus blanched, then his face turned a mottled red.

"You have no idea what it takes to stay on top." Marcus pointed a shaky finger at Adam, who couldn't decide whether the tremor was from fear or rage. "My dad expects me to be number one, and sometimes it means giving the system a shove my way. There's no way I'm letting him down, no matter what it takes."

Marcus seemed to falter, so Trent pushed on. "That just makes you a sad punk, not a great hero, Marcus. I actually feel sorry for you. I see where I've gone wrong and I'm going to fix it. You're stuck with your messed-up world." He moved closer. "And one more thing. *Stay away from Zoë.* If I hear of you sniffing around my sister again, so help me, I'll take you out." He limped haltingly to the door and opened it. "Now, get lost, you loser."

Marcus's face was frightening. It was twisted with rage and the insane look in his eyes gave Adam the creeps. He started to leave, then stopped, frowning as he studied the mantle.

Adam cursed under his breath as he saw that Marcus had spotted the tiny telltale red light on the camera.

"What the hell…?" Marcus walked over to the mantle and grabbed the camera. "You were video-taping this? You two think you're such clever little jerks." His teeth were clenched and his voice a low growl. "This is not acceptable behaviour, gentlemen. If this was what made you think you had any kind of control over me, I'd say you just lost your advantage." Ripping the tiny cassette out of the camera, he jammed it into his pocket, and moved toward Trent. "This isn't over, Kendall." With a lightning fast move, he punched Trent hard in the stomach.

Trent's breath whooshed out of his body. His bad leg gave, and he stumbled backward down the steps leading into the sunken living room. He fell heavily, wincing with pain as his right arm connected with the hard plank floor.

"Back off, Marcus!" Adam yelled, moving to his friend's aid.

Marcus sneered down at Trent who was cradling his injured wrist against his chest. "Oops, doesn't look like you can shift with that. I guess you two will be stuck here a while." He held up a key and shook it. "When I saw your bike here, Harlow, it ticked me off, so I took the liberty of removing the key. I noticed how gun-shy you are to get into a car with your friend, so I thought I'd make sure you were stuck here."

The colour drained from Adam's face. How did Marcus know about his fear?

Marcus paused, grinning at Adam. "Zoë gets very talkative once she's had a couple of my special drinks. And speaking of Zoë…" His eyes gleamed menacingly as he turned back to Trent. "If I remember right, she's home alone tonight while your parents are at some fancy charity function." He pulled a cell phone out of his leather jacket. "I'm supposed to call Gary to meet me. But after catching you two on that stupid camera trick, I feel like partying. I bet Gary wouldn't mind if Zoë comes along; in fact, he'd probably like it. The bouncers at the club know she's been out with me, so no one would believe her if she said she wasn't a willing date. With her brother falsely accusing me of selling drugs, it would look like the two Kendall kids were ganging up on poor little me."

Adam's temper boiled over. "Touch her, Dreger, and I'll hunt you down myself."

Marcus snorted derisively. "Like I'm afraid of you." He turned to go, then stopped. "Oh, and Harlow, just in case you sprout a backbone, I think I'll yank the spark plugs out of Trent's heap in the driveway, so this time you two can't interrupt my date." He laughed, leaving Adam and Trent staring after him.

Chapter 13

Trent frantically tried to stand. "We've got to warn Zoë!" He struggled awkwardly, then fell wincing from the pain. His face was a pasty white.

Adam knew if they didn't have wheels, Zoë was in serious jeopardy, but panicking wasn't going to help. "Calm down, we have to think. He's right about one thing." He helped Trent struggle to his feet. "Without the video, we have no proof. It's our word against his. If you go to the police and tell them about Marcus and the drugs that's one thing, but if he hurts Zoë and she accuses him too … After the scene at the club, it isn't going to look good." Adam picked up his coat. "I'll try my cell, but I don't think it's going to work this far out." Pulling the small phone out of his pocket, he flipped it open. "No service. Is there any other way to contact Zoë?"

Trent shook his head. "The phones here won't work without power, and we don't have a generator."

Adam thought a moment. "We have to get within

cell range to warn Zoë, and we have to do it before Marcus can call his twisted friend and have him scoop your sister." He knew what he would have to do. Trent couldn't drive a standard with his shifting arm out of commission. Adam's stomach lurched and a shudder ran down his back. He took a deep breath. "Trent, do you have the keys to the Evo?"

"The old man keeps a spare set for all the cars." Hobbling to the large roll-top desk, he yanked open a drawer and retrieved a set of keys. He tossed them to Adam. "Is it true what Marcus said about you not wanting to be in a car with me?"

Adam couldn't answer. The words stuck in his throat.

"I guess that explains why you got sick that first day you were in the car with me, and why you wanted Zoë to co-drive." A look of comprehension dawned on Trent's face as he moved stiffly toward the front door. "And I bet you deliberately put the Evo out of commission for that rally, didn't you?" His face was pale, making the raw flesh of the scar stand out. "I don't get it. Why?"

Adam couldn't speak. The guilt he'd been swallowing for so long rose into his throat and choked him. Silently, he opened the door and waited as Trent continued his strange gait out onto the veranda. Pausing for a second, Trent stared speechlessly at Adam, then continued on.

Deep in his friend's eyes, Adam had seen a pain that had nothing to do with his damaged wrist. Adam knew he couldn't lie any more. He was tired of feeling guilty. The words spilled out. "Trent, every time I thought of you and a rally car, I remembered the accident." Adam couldn't stop. His mouth had no rev-limiter and he was red-lining. "When I try to sleep, I have nightmares. All I can hear are your screams and all I can see are your terrible scars. That accident was my fault, and now you'll have to live with the consequences for the rest of your life." Tears stung his eyes. "Don't you understand? I did this to you. If I'd been able to control that car better, we wouldn't have crashed. I thought I was such a hotshot driver, and look what I did to you."

Trent halted his awkward movement down the veranda steps and his eyes grew wide. "All this time, you thought the crash was your fault? Look, Harlow, you didn't force me to get in that car. In fact, if I remember right, the whole thing was my idea. I thought it would be cool to take the car, and I was the one not wearing my seat belt." He continued toward the garage. "Besides, no one could have driven out of that gravel patch you hit."

Adam looked at him blankly, then followed. "What gravel patch?"

"The one hiding at the apex of that corner you missed, the one that made the car slide so far to the edge of the road. You never had a chance to save it after that." Trent turned to him. "I guess that's why they tell you to wear your seat belt; so you can walk away from stupid accidents like that one." He smiled sadly at Adam. "It wasn't your fault. I wish you'd talked to me about this a long time ago. I've learned that secrets usually lead to lies. I'm done with hiding my screw-ups. We're going to be friends for a long time, so you'd better put this guilt thing behind you." He pushed open the side door into the garage. "There's only one way out — the Powderface — so we know which way Marcus is headed. Let's go nail that scum."

Adam stared at the keys in his hand, then squeezed his fist tightly. "I've never driven the Evo. I hope I can handle it."

Trent laughed. "Forget the Evo. We're taking the STi!"

With his heart hammering in his chest, Adam followed Trent into the garage. He was light-headed as he stood in front of the bullet-fast car. He kept telling himself that he could do this, but his stomach wasn't listening.

Trent got in and hit the automatic garage door opener as Adam gingerly settled himself behind the wheel. His hands went numb and he started to sweat. Gritting his teeth, he shut his eyes and whispered hoarsely, "I can do this. *I can do this!*" His stomach heaved and he shoved the door open, barely managing to get his head outside of the expensive car before throwing up.

"Sure, you can," Trent agreed ruefully.

Fighting a strong urge to get out of the car, Adam waited until the black blotches floating in front of his eyes cleared. He focused on Zoë, alone and unsuspecting at home. He had to stop Marcus.

Two helmets sat neatly on a sheaf of stapled papers behind the seat. "We're not going anywhere until you have one of these on. If we crash, I want to know I did everything I could to protect you," Adam said, jamming one of the expensive helmets onto Trent's head. He did up the chinstrap, then put his own on, and flipped the mike switches. Fumbling, he fastened both of their seat belts, pulling the harness straps snug.

Reaching behind the seat, he retrieved the papers. He checked the title, then handed them to Trent. "I think these pace notes for the Powderface will come in handy. You yell out directions and I'll try not to fall off the road." His lip bent into a quirky smile. "Do you want a Gravol before flying with me?"

Trent grinned back. "No worries. I'm used to turbulence."

With an unsteady hand, Adam turned the key in the ignition and the STi roared to life. He gripped the gearshift and shoved it into first. His breathing was ragged and his hands tingled on the wheel.

"You can do this," Trent said encouragingly.

Whispering a silent prayer that his friend was right, Adam slipped the clutch.

Chapter 14

Adam wasn't sure his numbed body would do what he told it. His legs were rubbery as his foot came down on the accelerator. It seemed like a lifetime and not a couple of weeks since he and Trent had last sat side by side in a rally car.

The last rays of the dying sun struggled feebly to light the gloomy sky. Then the bruised clouds closed and the world was shrouded in darkness.

Adam focused his gaze as far down the road as possible. This was the key to a fast drive and he knew it. He kept his breathing even as the trees flashed by, slowly at first, then faster and faster. The seat wrapped comfortably around him and the familiar feel of clutch, gas, and brake beneath his feet made the knot in his stomach start to loosen. The rain broke just as they reached the bottom of the drive.

"Right turn! Straight, five hundred metres, four left!" Trent yelled, struggling to follow the pace notes on his lap.

First the brakes, then a flick of the steering wheel and Adam had the rear end of the car swinging out; quickly, he cranked the wheel back and hit the gas to pull them around the sharp turn. Cursing the rookie mistake, he realized he should have downshifted before he entered the corner, but it was too late now. The car slowed dramatically and he was forced to blip the throttle, shifting rapidly to keep the revs up. The car responded instantly.

In a shower of scattered pebbles, the STi leaped forward down the road. The rain was a solid slate sheet that turned the windshield into a blurry mess. "Where's the damn wiper switch?" Adam yelled, not taking his eyes off the road. He wished he'd had time to familiarize himself with the controls before they'd left.

Trent reached over and flipped the wipers on. The windshield immediately cleared, showing the open road ahead of them.

"Marcus has driven this road too." Relying on muscle memory to finesse the wheel correctly, Adam deftly manoeuvred around a fallen tree. "He's got a good lead so, if we want to overtake him, we'll have to really haul." He was already calculating how hard he could push the car before he was over the line, before the car was driving him instead of the other way around.

At the performance driving course, his instructor had told him the best way to control the car and end up a winner was to drive only eight tenths of your capability. "Great drivers don't react; they anticipate," had been the instructor's parting advice to Adam, and he'd been right. If you were reacting to a situation in a car, then it was already too late.

Adam tried to anticipate now, to stay in control. Zoë's safety depended on it. The STi hit a particularly vicious pothole, slamming them with a bone-jarring thump.

"Ow, jeez!" Trent winced as he tried to protect his mangled wrist. "This thing definitely needs softer suspension!" He blew out a breath noisily. "Don't forget, Marcus doesn't know we're after him. We, my fast friend, have the element of surprise and the fact that, until he sees us in his mirrors, the creepoid won't be too inclined to thrash that Bimmer on these rough roads."

They sped down the twisting mountain road as Trent called out directions to Adam. "Six right…" They were through the fast corner before Adam had time to think about what he'd just done. "Three left…" Adam braked for the tighter left turn.

Mud splashed up over the hood and splattered the windshield with a sludgy mess. The wipers struggled to clear the sticky crud as Adam fumbled for the washer fluid switch.

He was starting to get a feel for the car. Jorge had done a super job of complementing all the components, which made the STi incredibly responsive. Adam had never driven a car like this. The road was extremely rough, and only their safety harnesses kept them in their seats, but still he refused to back off. The trees were a dark green blur as Adam concentrated on keeping his driving smooth. The adrenaline rushed in his system, but this time it was a good thing.

"On your left, three deer!" Trent yelled into his mike, rattling Adam's eardrums.

"I see them!" Adam sang out.

"Straight, fifty metres … hairpin left … straight ten metres … chicane. Damn!" Trent cursed as the Subaru hit a large cobble in the road, and the rock rumbled ominously off the skid plate.

Adam pushed the car and himself even harder, as he concentrated on doing everything right. There was a sudden flash of silver in the trees ahead. "It's Marcus! He's nearly out of the chicane." Adam swung the car into the hairpin just as Marcus's car emerged and started up a steep incline.

"He'll have us in his mirrors in a second," Trent said, watching the BMW. "Let's hope he decides to give up the chase. There's a whole lot of vertical drop coming up after the next sharp left, and there are no guard rails out here."

Trent sounded extremely nervous to Adam. He knew what that was like. "I thought you said you could handle the turbulence!" Adam joked as he tried to ease the tension. He knew the real problem was Marcus's friend. If Marcus made it into cell range, then their problem doubled. He thought of Zoë, and came out of the chicane with all four tires clawing for traction.

The STi hit the bottom of the incline and Adam scanned the long steep hill, expecting to see Marcus's car. It was gone. "He couldn't have reached the top already. We were only two seconds behind him. Where is he?"

They blasted up the rutted slope and started into the tight left turn at the top. Adam noticed that the road narrowed where the outside edge had eroded away. He knew it was a steep drop off, because all he could see were low-lying clouds, and no sturdy trees to catch them if he screwed up.

Without warning, he was startled by the glare of headlights in his mirrors. The BMW shot out of a cut line that intersected the road. The sleek silver car quickly closed on the STi, smashing into the left side of their back bumper.

"Man, looks like Marcus isn't worried about his insurance premiums going up!" Trent yelled, grabbing for something to hold on to.

The sudden impact spun the bright blue car, sending it careening toward the outer edge of the road.

Adam fought to regain control, but the back end continued to slide. His breath caught in his throat as his mind flashed back to the night of the accident. It was going to happen all over again!

Knuckles white on the steering wheel, Adam fought to subdue the car before they went over. Everything happened in slow motion. The STi shuddered as he cranked the wheel, then stabbed the gas, trying to correct the deadly skid.

The muscles in his arms ached as Adam fought the twitchy car. He had to use exactly the right amount of steering input to the front wheels or the car would over-correct and spin the other way. Sweat ran into his eyes.

Marcus sped by on the inside.

After what seemed a lifetime, the car reluctantly began doing what it was told. Adam caught the skid and held the STi under control. As the Subaru began to straighten out, he unwound the wheel and exited the corner, full on the gas.

As he steadied the car and his nerves, Adam caught a glimpse of the BMW's tail lights disappearing around the next bend in the road.

"That was too close!" Trent gingerly touched his wrist, which had swollen to twice its normal size. "Adam, you okay, man?"

Adam released the breath he'd been holding. "No sweat!" Then, like a vulture circling in the desert, a grim thought occurred to Adam. "Marcus has driven this road. He knew there was a huge drop-off on that corner." He glanced over at his friend meaningfully. "Trent, he tried to take us out *permanently*."

"That proves he's flat-out crazy!" Trent was becoming extremely agitated. "We have to stop him. There's no telling what he'll do to Zoë if he gets his hands on her."

Adam heard real terror in Trent's voice. They had to stop Marcus and, with a sinking feeling, he realized he knew how to do it. He had no choice, but when he thought of what would happen next, his guts twisted and his throat closed until he could hardly suck in a lungful of air. Then he thought of Zoë and his hands tightened on the wheel.

"Don't worry, Trent. I know how to stop him." Adam punched the accelerator and the agile car shot forward. He was totally focused on catching the BMW and was rewarded by a brief glimpse of the silver car on the road ahead.

"Do you remember when we used to ice race?" Adam asked calmly as he blasted through a washed-out section like it was new blacktop.

Trent glanced at him and frowned, confused. "Yeah. What are you getting at?"

The STi was slowly reeling the BMW in. Adam downshifted as he handled a tight corner perfectly. "Remember how that jerk Colin Jablonski used me for brakes in that race in Edmonton?"

Trent thought for a moment, then understanding lit his face. "There's a nice right-handed sweeper coming up. It should do nicely, but you'll have to explain to Jorge why you deliberately banged up his car."

They crested a rise and Adam saw the fast right-hander waiting ahead. "Hold on. This is going to hurt."

Adam shoved his foot to the floor and the STi accelerated hard.

As Marcus slid the BMW sideways through the corner, the back end pivoted around to the outside.

Adam judged where to clip his apex and, taking

a deep breath, started his own fast slide. With a satisfying crunch, the driver's side of the STi smacked up against the passenger side of the BMW at exactly the right spot.

The impact caused the BMW to fire off the corner at full speed, skidding it into the rough ground at the edge of the road. The fender slammed into a large boulder and bits of expensive German engineering flew off the splintered body in all directions. The car rocked on two wheels, perilously close to rolling over, then finally came to rest against a mammoth pine. Clouds of white steam billowed out from under the mangled hood.

"Jeez. Nicely done, Adam!" Trent hooted as Adam slammed on the brakes. "I think Marcus just landed himself in a world of hurt!"

"Grab the fire extinguisher, just in case. I'll get him out!"

Adam punched the release on his seat belt and bolted out of the STi. His heart pounded as he sprinted toward the smashed BMW. In his mind's eye, he could see Trent's broken and crushed body lying in a pool of his own blood.

Marcus remained strapped behind the wheel, not moving. Blood streamed from a deep gash on his forehead and he was deathly pale. Icy fingers squeezed the air out of Adam's lungs. His worst nightmare was back. Because he was driving a rally car, someone else had suffered. He'd killed Marcus Dreger.

The air bags had deployed and Adam could

smell leaking gas. His hands shook as he yanked open the door and released Marcus's seat belt, then dragged the unresponsive body out of the mangled car. Kneeling beside Marcus, Adam stared down at his still, bloodied face and prayed it wasn't as bad as it looked.

A noise made Adam look up. Trent was hustling toward him, fire extinguisher at the ready. As he watched his friend, Adam realized Trent's limp barely registered anymore. It was simply part of who Trent was, like the washed-out green eyes or his slightly uneven front teeth, a small part of a whole person.

Some part of Adam's brain recognized that the rain had stopped and how fresh and clean the air smelled. Absently, he wondered if he was going into shock.

Remembering his first-aid training, he knew he had to check Marcus for a pulse. Tentatively, Adam pressed two fingers against the wax-coloured flesh on the battered teen's neck. The skin was cold to his touch and he couldn't feel the telltale thump of a heartbeat. "Please don't let this be happening," he whispered a desperate prayer, pressing harder to find the missing pulse.

Marcus twitched, then groaned.

Adam closed his eyes. "Thank God!" He went weak with relief. Marcus wasn't dead! He hadn't killed him!

Trent stopped when he saw Marcus, and Adam took a deep breath as he tried to control the quaver in his voice. "He's in bad shape. We've got to get him to a hospital."

As he stared down at Marcus's bloody face and broken body, Trent shrugged. "I vote we leave him here to rot, just another roadkill."

"What!" Adam's head snapped up in startled surprise. As a slow grin cracked Trent's scarred face, Adam saw he wasn't serious.

Trent set the fire extinguisher down and raised his good hand in an exaggerated gesture of surrender. "Okay, okay, we'll haul his sorry butt to the hospital, but it's going to be pretty cramped in that STi."

Together, they managed to get Marcus's unconscious body loaded into the car.

Adam did up his seat belt, feeling more at peace with himself than he had in a long time. He was no longer nervous about being in a rally car with Trent, his best friend who happened to have ADHD and who wore his old war wounds like a comfortable pair of patched jeans.

In fact, Adam was very glad his friend was along to hold on to Marcus's limp body. It was going to be a fast ride.

Chapter 15

Emergency personnel wheeled Marcus away as a doctor checked Trent's wrist.

"It looks like it's sprained. We'd better get some x-rays to make sure. Don't worry, we'll have you back playing the piano in no time." The doctor winked reassuringly at Trent, then patted his shoulder before leaving the small curtained cubicle.

"Did you call my folks?" Trent asked Adam as soon as the doctor had left.

"They're on the way. I called my own parents too, in case they get a call from the police about the accident. It would freak them out. The officer outside said he'd notify Detective Dreger." Adam pointed toward the waiting room where a blue-uniformed policeman was busy with the accident report. "He said Marcus's mom lives in Edmonton. I guess it could be tough not having a mom around when your dad is a hard-nosed cop."

Trent grimaced in pain. "It doesn't clear him on

being a number-one jerk. Adam, he's trying to derail my life! If I lose that scholarship, I don't know what I'll do. Not to mention how he threatened Zoë!"

He ran his fingers along the edge of the sheet, pulling viciously at any loose thread he found. "But the worst will be if my being a screw-up hurts my dad's chances at running for office. He's a tough guy to live around and I never let him forget it, but deep down I know he's fair to me. I guess I never wanted to admit that because it would mean I'm an even worse screw-up than I'd thought.

"I know now that I'm my own worst enemy. I make poor choices and never give my dad the benefit of the doubt. He's put himself on the line time and time again, knowing I'll mess up the next chance I get. This is going to kill him."

Adam took a step closer to the bed and clamped his hand down over Trent's arm, stopping him from torturing the sheet. "First, you are not a screw-up. And second, why does this have to be a bad thing? You made a mistake in the beginning, but you tried to fix it. Marcus wouldn't let you, in fact, he was taking you down a path which would have put you behind bars for sure." He smiled at his friend before releasing his arm. "Your dad's a lawyer, for crying out loud. He'll weigh all the evidence fairly and I know he'll acquit you."

"How can you be so sure?" Trent asked, leaning back against the bed and covering his eyes with his forearm.

"Simple," Adam smiled. "Because he loves you."

There was a commotion in the hallway, and then the curtains parted, admitting Trent's mom, his dad, and Zoë.

"What's going on here, Trent?" Mr. Kendall began. "Adam called and said something about Marcus, drugs, and an accident in the STi. He also insisted we bring Zoë with us." He stopped, his glance taking in Trent's wrist, and then he shook his head. "I'm sorry, son. I've been so worried since Adam called. First things first — are you okay?"

"Yeah, nothing much." Trent tried to sound casual, but Adam heard the pain in his voice.

Trent's mom gave her son a hug. "Has the doctor been in?"

"Yes, and he thinks the wrist is just sprained." Trent lifted his injured arm up. "I'm going to x-ray to make sure there are no broken bones."

"What did Marcus have to do with this?" Zoë asked, a confused look on her pretty face.

Trent turned to Adam, who gave him the thumbs up. "Sit down everyone. Dad, I've got something to tell you." Together, Trent and Adam explained what had happened. As the incredible story unfolded, Mr. Kendall was at first skeptical, then angry, and finally thoughtful.

"I want you to know how sorry I am," Trent finished as his gaze rested on his father.

Adam thought his friend's eyes were suspiciously shiny in the corners.

Trent went on, "When I was first diagnosed with ADHD, I was so angry at everything and everyone, especially you. It was as though you thought if you bought enough doctors, pills, or tutors, you could make it go away and I'd be the son you always wanted. I was hurt. I decided to show you I knew what I was doing and didn't need the stupid drugs. I thought selling them to Marcus was a great way to get back at you, but all I did was to set myself up."

Mr. Kendall's face fell. "Trent, I only did those things because I wanted to help you. I admit son, I didn't consult you. I'm used to making decisions for people, finding the right solution. I handled things in the only way I knew." He searched his son's face. "Despite what you believe, I don't have such a giant ego as to think I have the solution for all of life's problems. If I'm in over my head, I send for reinforcements. I hire the doctors and the trainers. And yes, I was willing to put you on drugs because I thought I was helping."

Trent ran his good hand through his tangled hair. "After I was on the Ritalin for a while, I started noticing changes in myself. I liked the way things were going. For the first time in a long while, I felt like I was in control. But by then, it was too late. Marcus had his hooks in me and wasn't about to let go. I had to manufacture symptoms so I could get enough medicine for me and still supply Marcus. He kept asking for more. Then when I won the scholarship to McGill, he found out how good I was at chemistry and decided I could build him better drugs with more street value.

"I don't know what I would have done if Adam hadn't persuaded me to tell Marcus to get lost. I didn't want to build the stuff, but Marcus said no one would believe me if I went to the cops. I'd sold the Ritalin to him in front of a witness and then assaulted him at the club. He also threatened to expose my past and that old pot bust." The tears that had threatened spilled over. "I would have come off as a first-class junior drug dealer and, Dad, it would have finished your political career before it even got started. But Adam persuaded me that it had gone too far. He said we had to do the right thing, that I couldn't go on being a slave to Marcus, but when I said no, the creep threatened Zoë. I knew then that no matter what it cost, he had to be stopped in a big way."

Trent's father lay his hand gently on his son's shoulder. "Let me look into this. I need more facts before I can make any conclusions or recommendations, but I want you to remember one thing. Whatever happens, we'll get through this *together*."

Adam thought he saw something flicker across Zoë's face. Then she stepped forward.

"Dad, some of this is my fault. I went out with Marcus to prove I was old enough to make my own decisions and…" She hesitated. "Also because, since the accident, I felt like I was invisible. Litt Zoë, the good girl who never got into any trouble.

guess I thought if I messed up, I'd get to share some of Trent's spotlight."

Mr. Kendall shook his head, surprised. "Zoë, honey, your mother and I have never ignored you. We've tried to give you your own space because we didn't want you to feel smothered. I was so happy when you started asking about rallying because it gave us something in common. I was proud of both my kids taking an interest in the sport, a real Kendall family thing."

Zoë moved into her father's arms. Mrs. Kendall took some tissues out of her purse and dabbed at her eyes as she held one out to her daughter. Zoë started to giggle. "Oh, Mom…" She took the proffered tissue and wiped her nose.

Adam stepped forward. "I think this might help you make your decision, Mr. Kendall." He pulled the tiny cassette out of his pocket and handed it to Trent's dad.

Mr. Kendall raised an eyebrow at Adam. "I'm guessing this is Exhibit A."

Adam smiled confidently. "I think you'll like what you see."

Trent looked at him questioningly and Adam shrugged. "I took it out of Marcus's pocket before we loaded him into the STi."

Trent took a deep breath, then turned back to his father. "One more thing, Dad. Last time I got into serious trouble, I had you hush it up, make it go away. I don't want to do that this time. I'm going to make the slate clean myself. I messed up and I want to do whatever it takes to put it right. No more secrets."

The senior Kendall smiled at his son. "That's about the best thing a father or a lawyer could hear. Trent, don't worry about my career, just be concerned with yours. The truth isn't what scares me in the political ring." Just then, the porter came to take Trent for his x-rays. "I'll be here when you get back, son."

As Trent's parents talked, Adam and Zoë left to get a drink from the vending machine in the waiting room. It was then that they saw the police car race into the parking lot and screech to a halt, lights flashing. Marcus's dad rushed into the emergency room and went straight to the reception desk.

"My son, Marcus Dreger, was brought in a while ago. It was an MVA, a motor vehicle accident. Where is he?" Adam saw the big man's pale face. Worry lines etched the corners of his wide mouth.

"He's gone to have some x-rays done. If you'd like to have a seat, I can call you when they bring him back." The pretty, young ward clerk pointed to the waiting room with her pen.

"Look, my name is James Dreger, *Detective* James Dreger. Is there any way we can speed this whole thing up? I don't want my son left in some hallway while he waits his turn for an x-ray. needs them now, do them *now*."

The ward clerk's smile was chiselled in stone.

"Your son will be back shortly, Detective Dreger. Please have a seat."

Adam saw Mr. Kendall coming out of the small cubicle where Trent had been. Marcus's dad spotted him at the same time. He stormed over and pointed an accusing finger. "That drugged-up kid of yours tried to kill my boy! It wasn't enough that he beat him up at a club, he had to try and finish the job. He's a thug and I'm going to make sure he's put away. I did some investigating and have uncovered his dirty history." His tone was hard, his meaning clear. "Despite your best efforts to hide the fact, that kid's been into drugs before and I'm going to make sure it's brought out into the open."

Trent's father stared back at Detective Dreger, then drew himself up to his full height, looking every centimetre a top-notch criminal lawyer. "My son is more than willing to account for what he's done. What concerns me, *Detective Dreger*, is your son. You're right. We all have skeletons in our closets. After you phoned about the problem at the club, I did some investigating..." His tone became steel. "I called a couple of friends of mine on the force and discovered your boy has some serious skeletons of his own. He's been in trouble with the law several times. You used a couple of favours you were owed to have the charges dropped, or to make crucial evidence mysteriously disappear. The Towes punk he's hanging around with has been involved with drug trafficking before and should be behind bars."

Counsellor Kendall took a step toward Detective Dreger. "Before you start throwing accusations around, I suggest you get your own house in order." He shook his head slowly, relenting a little. "This is a bad situation and we need to make it right. We both want what's best for our sons."

Adam saw Detective Dreger flinch, then back down in front of the truth. Marcus had been doing illegal stuff for years, but this time he wouldn't be getting away with it.

Adam felt great. Trent was going to love hearing this. His marijuana misdemeanour was nothing compared to Marcus Dreger's list of accomplishments!

He turned to Zoë, feeling a lot less apprehensive about Trent's future. "Let's go sit and wait for your brother." He reached down and took her hand, holding it tightly in his. Zoë squeezed his back as together they walked to the cubicle.

After what seemed like hours, Trent was wheeled in from x-ray to where his family and Adam were waiting. His arm was heavily bandaged and he had a sling around his neck. "The wrist is badly sprained, but the doctors say they can have me back rallying in no time," Trent said, with relief. "Has anyone heard how Marcus is doing?"

"I asked the nurse and she said he'll be fine," Adam reported. "He has a concussion, and they're going to keep him in for observation, but he should be out in a couple of days." Trent's expression started to falter and his face clouded over at the thought of Marcus going free. Adam hurried on. "But we haven't told you the punchline. Wait till you hear this…" He proceeded to tell Trent about Marcus and his less than stellar track record.

"What this means, son, is that the crown prosecutor will be far more interested in Marcus Dreger's involvement than in yours." Mr. Kendall looked at his son and Adam could see something new in his eyes — trust. "When we tell the judge how you want to make reparation, I know that will go a long way in your favour. You might be on probation for a short time, but I think things are going to be all right."

Adam saw a smile sneak onto his friend's face and he knew that Trent's relationship with his father had changed. Every kid messes up, it was part of life, but Adam figured from now on if Trent did screw up, it would be from making honest mistakes that he and his dad could fix together.

He thought about Marcus and his father. Having to be number one all the time didn't leave any room to be a normal kid. Who knows what Marcus would have ended up doing to keep his father's love? Whatever it was, it was too high a price tag for something that should have been given freely.

Adam suddenly appreciated his own dad a whole lot more.

"Hey, speaking of rallying…" Zoë began, bringing Adam's attention back to the conversation. "The Rocky Mountain Rally is scheduled in two weeks.

Trent, you won't be able to drive but…"

A gleam came into her eyes that made Adam nervous. "By then I'll have finished the performance driving school I'm enrolled in," she said, smiling at their surprised faces. "I've been saving my allowance to pay for it. No one knew because this was important to me, and I didn't want a certain brother saying rallying is just for boys." She stuck her tongue out at Trent, who grinned back. "And I think Adam and I would make a good team. Of course it would only be until you can pilot the Evo again yourself, Trent," she said innocently, then she turned to Adam. "What do you say, Adam? Do you want to team up? I'd be the best damn co-driver you've ever had."

"Dad, she can't drive the Evo. She's gruesome with a gearshift!" Trent lamented. "Adam, say you won't do it!"

Behind the melodramatic appeal, Adam saw the smile Trent was trying to hide.

Mr. Kendall rubbed his chin thoughtfully as he considered his daughter's proposal. "Now, Trent, you know your sister isn't that bad behind the wheel. I've ridden with her myself. Adam has a lot of talent and he'd be the one driving the Evo, not Zoë … at least in the beginning."

Mrs. Kendall rolled her eyes. "Just what I need. Another rally driver in the family."

Adam smiled at Zoë. The idea of being alone in a car with Zoë Kendall for hours on end doing what he loved to do best made Adam's stomach give a little lurch. But this time he knew it was a good thing — in fact, a really great thing!

He had beaten his racing fear and knew that nothing was going to hold him back from his dreams. From now on, his future was going to be lived at full throttle.